The Life of Nancy

The Life of Nancy

Sarah Orne Jewett

MINT EDITIONS

The Life of Nancy was first published in 1895.

This edition published by Mint Editions 2021.

ISBN 9781513279862 | E-ISBN 9781513284880

Published by Mint Editions®

 MINT
EDITIONS

minteditionbooks.com

Publishing Director: Jennifer Newens
Design & Production: Rachel Lopez Metzger
Project Manager: Micaela Clark
Typesetting: Westchester Publishing Services

Contents

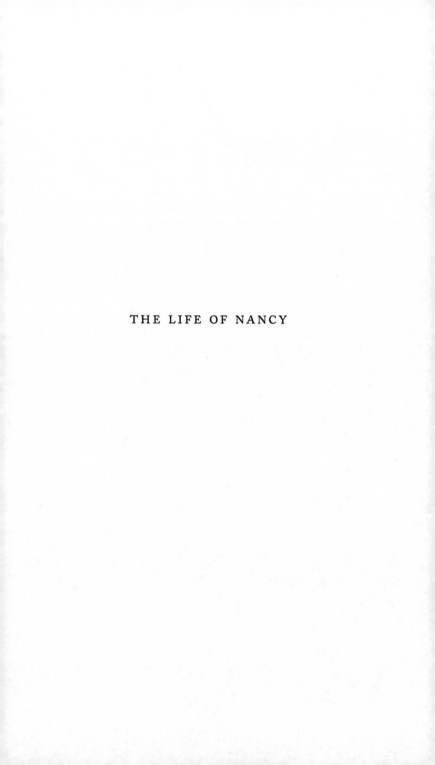

THE LIFE OF NANCY

I

The wooded hills and pastures of eastern Massachusetts are so close to Boston that from upper windows of the city, looking westward, you can see the tops of pine-trees and orchard-boughs on the high horizon. There is a rustic environment on the landward side; there are old farmhouses at the back of Milton Hill and beyond Belmont which look as unchanged by the besieging suburbs of a great city as if they were forty miles from even its borders. Now and then, in Boston streets, you can see an old farmer in his sleigh or farm wagon as if you saw him in a Berkshire village. He seems neither to look up at the towers nor down at any fashionable citizens, but goes his way alike unconscious of seeing or being seen.

On a certain day a man came driving along Beacon Street, who looked bent in the shoulders, as if his worn fur cap were too heavy for head and shoulders both. This type of the ancient New England farmer in winter twitched the reins occasionally, like an old woman, to urge the steady white horse that plodded along as unmindful of his master's suggestions as of the silver-mounted harnesses that passed them by. Both horse and driver appeared to be conscious of sufficient wisdom, and even worth, for the duties of life; but all this placidity and self-assurance were in sharp contrast to the eager excitement of a pretty, red-cheeked girl who sat at the driver's side. She was as sensitive to every new impression as they were dull. Her face bloomed out of a round white hood in such charming fashion that those who began to smile at an out-of-date equipage were interrupted by a second and stronger instinct, and paid the homage that one must always pay to beauty.

It was a bitter cold morning. The great sleighbells on the horse's shaggy neck jangled along the street, and seemed to still themselves as they came among the group of vehicles that were climbing the long hill by the Common.

As the sleigh passed a clubhouse that stands high on the slope, a young man who stood idly behind one of the large windows made a hurried step forward, and his sober face relaxed into a broad, delighted smile; then he turned quickly, and presently appearing at the outer door, scurried down the long flight of steps to the street, fastening the top buttons of his overcoat by the way. The old sleigh, with its worn buffalo skin hanging unevenly over the back, was only a short distance up the street, but its pursuer found trouble in gaining much upon the steady gait of the white horse. He ran two or three steps now and then, and was almost close enough to speak as he drew near to the pavement by the State House. The pretty girl was looking up with wonder and delight, but in another moment they went briskly on, and it was not until a long pause had to be made at the blocked crossing of Tremont Street that the chase was ended.

The wonders of a first visit to Boston were happily continued to Miss Nancy Gale in the sudden appearance at her side of a handsome young gentleman. She put out a most cordial and warm hand from her fitch muff, and her acquaintance noticed with pleasure the white knitted mitten that protected it from the weather. He had not yet found time to miss the gloves left behind at the club, but the warm little mitten was very comfortable to his fingers.

"I was just thinking—I hoped I should see you, when I was starting to come in this morning," she said, with an eager look of pleasure; then, growing shy after the unconscious joy of the first moment, "Boston is a pretty big place, isn't it?"

"We all think so," said Tom Aldis with fine candor. "It seems odd to see you here."

"Uncle Ezra, this is Mr. Aldis that I have been telling you about, who was down at our place so long in the fall," explained Nancy, turning to look appealingly at her stern companion. "Mr. Aldis had to remain with a friend who had sprained his ankle. Is Mr. Carew quite well now?" she turned again to ask.

"Oh yes," answered Tom. "I saw him last week; he's in New York this winter. But where are you staying, Nancy?" he asked eagerly, with a hopeful glance at uncle Ezra. "I should like to take you somewhere this afternoon. This is your first visit, isn't it? Couldn't you go to see Rip Van Winkle to-morrow? It's the very best thing there is just now. Jefferson's playing this week."

"Our folks ain't in the habit of attending theatres, sir," said uncle Ezra, checking this innocent plan as effectually as an untracked horse-car was stopping traffic in the narrow street. He looked over his shoulder to see if there were any room to turn, but was disappointed.

Tom Aldis gave a glance, also, and was happily reassured; the street was getting fuller behind them every moment. "I beg you to excuse me, sir," he said gallantly to the old man. "Do you think of anything else that Miss Gale ought to see? There is the Art Museum, if she hasn't been there already; all the pictures and statues and Egyptian things, you know."

There was much deference and courtesy in the young man's behavior to his senior. Uncle Ezra responded by a less suspicious look at him, but seemed to be considering this new proposition before he spoke. Uncle Ezra was evidently of the opinion that while it might be a misfortune to be an old man, it was a fault to be a young one and good looking where girls were concerned. "Miss Gale's father and mother showed me so much kindness," Tom explained, seizing his moment of advantage, "I should like to be of some use: it may not be convenient for you to come into town again in this cold weather."

"Our folks have plenty to do all the time, that's a fact," acknowledged uncle Ezra less grimly, while Nancy managed to show the light of a very knowing little smile. "I don't know but she'd like to have a city man show her about, anyways. 'T ain't but four miles an' a half out to our place, the way we come, but while this weather holds I don't calculate to get into Boston more'n once a week. I fetch all my stuff in to the Quincy Market myself, an' I've got to come in day after to-morrow mornin', but not till late, with a barrel o' nice winter pears I've been a-savin'. I can set the barrel right for'ard in the sleigh here, and I do' know but I can fetch Nancy as well as not. But how'd ye get home, Nancy? Could ye walk over to our place from the Milton depot, or couldn't ye?"

"Why, of course I could!" answered his niece, with a joy calmed by discretion.

"'T ain't but a mile an' three quarters; 't won't hurt a State 'o Maine girl," said the old man, smiling under his great cap, so that his cold, shrewd eyes suddenly grew blue and boyish. "I know all about ye now, Mr. Aldis; I used to be well acquainted with your grandfather. Much obliged to you. Yes, I'll fetch Nancy. I'll leave her right up there to the Missionary Building, corner o' Somerset Street. She can wait in the bookstore; it's liable to be open early. After I get through business to-day, I'm goin' to leave the hoss, an' let her see Faneuil Hall, an' the market o' course, and I don't know but we shall stop in to the Old South Church; or you can show her that, an' tell her about any other curiosities, if we don't have time."

Nancy looked radiant, and Tom Aldis accepted his trust with satisfaction. At that moment the blockade was over and teams began to move.

"Not if it rains!" said uncle Ezra, speaking distinctly over his shoulder as they started. "Otherwise expect her about eight or a little"—but the last of the sentence was lost.

Nancy looked back and nodded from the tangle to Tom, who stood on the curbstone with his hands in his pockets. Her white hood bobbed out of sight the next moment in School Street behind a great dray.

"Good gracious! eight o'clock!" said Tom, a little daunted, as he walked quickly up the street. As he passed the Missionary Building and the bookstore, he laughed aloud; but as he came near the clubhouse again, in this victorious retreat, he looked up at a window of one of the pleasant old houses, and then obeyed the beckoning nod of an elderly relative who seemed to have been watching for his return.

"Tom," said she, as he entered the library, "I insist upon it that I am not curious by nature or by habit, but what in the world made you chase that funny old horse and sleigh?"

"A pretty girl," said Tom frankly.

II

The second morning after this unexpected interview was sunshiny enough, and as cold as January could make it. Tom Aldis, being young and gay, was apt to keep late hours at this season, and the night before had been the night of a Harvard assembly. He was the kindest-hearted fellow in the world, but it was impossible not to feel a little glum and sleepy as he hurried toward the Missionary Building. The sharp air had urged uncle Ezra's white horse beyond his customary pace, so that the old sleigh was already waiting, and uncle Ezra himself was flapping his chilled arms and tramping to and fro impatiently.

"Cold mornin'!" he said. "She's waitin' for you in there. I wanted to be sure you'd come. Now I'll be off. I've got them pears well covered, but I expect they may be touched. Nancy counted on comin', an' I'd just as soon she'd have a nice time. Her cousin's folks'll see her to the depot," he added as he drove away, and Tom nodded reassuringly from the bookstore door.

Nancy looked up eagerly from beside a counter full of gayly bound books, and gave him a speechless and grateful good-morning.

"I'm getting some presents for the little boys," she informed him. "They're great hands to read. This one's all about birds, for Sam, and I don't know but this Life o' Napoleon'll please Asa as much as anything. When I waked up this morning I felt homesick. I couldn't see anything out o' the window that I knew. I'm a real home body."

"I should like to send the boys a present, myself," said Tom. "What do you think about jack-knives?"

"Asa'd rather have readin' matter; he ain't got the use for a knife that some boys have. Why, you're real good!" said Nancy.

"And your mother,—can't I send her something that she would like?" asked Tom kindly.

"She liked all those things that you and Mr. Carew sent at Christmas time. We had the loveliest time opening the bundles. You oughtn't to think o' doing anything more. I wish you'd help me pick out a nice large-print Bible for grandma; she's always wishing for a large-print Bible, and her eyes fail her a good deal."

Tom Aldis was not very fond of shopping, but this pious errand did not displease him in Nancy's company. A few minutes later, when they went out into the cold street, he felt warm and cheerful, and carried under his arm the flat parcel which held a large-print copy of the Scriptures and the little boys' books. Seeing Nancy again seemed to carry his thoughts back to East Rodney, as if he had been born and brought up there as well as she. The society and scenery of the little coast town were so simple and definite in their elements that one easily acquired a feeling of citizenship; it was like becoming acquainted with a friendly individual. Tom had an intimate knowledge, gained from several weeks' residence, with Nancy's whole world.

The long morning stretched before them like a morning in far Cathay, and they stepped off down the street toward the Old South Church, which had been omitted from uncle Ezra's scheme of entertainment by reason of difficulty in leaving the horse. The discovery that the door would not be open for nearly another hour only involved a longer walk among the city streets, and the asking and answering of many questions about the East Rodney neighbors, and the late autumn hunting and fishing which, with some land interests of his father's, had first drawn Tom to that part of the country. He had known enough of the rest of the world to appreciate the little community of fishermen-farmers, and while his friend Carew was but a complaining captive with a sprained ankle, Tom Aldis entered into the spirit of rural life with great zest; in fact he now remembered some boyish gallantries with a little uneasiness, and looked to Nancy to befriend him. It was easy for a man of twenty-two to arrive at an almost brotherly affection for such a person as Nancy; she was so discreet and so sincerely affectionate.

Nancy looked up at him once or twice as they walked along, and her face glowed with happy pride. "I'd just like to have Addie Porter see me now!" she exclaimed, and gave Tom a straightforward look to which he promptly responded.

"Why?" he asked.

Nancy drew a long breath of relief, and began to smile.

"Oh, nothing," she answered; "only she kept telling me that you wouldn't have much of anything to say to me, if I should happen to meet you anywhere up to Boston. I knew better. I guess you're all right, aren't you, about that?" She spoke with sudden impulse, but there was something in her tone that made Tom blush a little.

"Why, yes," he answered. "What do you mean, Nancy?"

"We won't talk about it now while we're full of seeing things, but I've got something to say by and by," said the girl soberly.

"You're very mysterious," protested Tom, taking the bundle under his other arm, and piloting her carefully across the street.

Nancy said no more. The town was more interesting now that it seemed to have waked up, and her eyes were too busy. Everything proved delightful that day, from the recognition of business signs familiar to her through newspaper advertisements, to the Great Organ, and the thrill which her patriotic heart experienced in a second visit to Faneuil Hall. They found the weather so mild that they pushed on to Charlestown, and went to the top of the monument, which Tom had not done since he was a very small boy. After this they saw what else they could of historic Boston, on the fleetest and lightest of feet, and talked all the way, until they were suddenly astonished to hear the bells in all the steeples ring at noon.

"Oh dear, my nice mornin' 's all gone," said Nancy regretfully. "I never had such a beautiful time in all my life!"

She looked quite beautiful herself as she spoke: her eyes shone with lovely light and feeling, and her cheeks were bright with color like a fresh-bloomed rose, but for the first time that day she was wistful and sorry.

"Oh, you needn't go back yet!" said Tom. "I've nothing in the world to do."

"Uncle Ezra thought I'd better go up to cousin Snow's in Revere Street. I'm afraid she'll be all through dinner, but never mind. They thought I'd better go there on mother's account; it's her cousin, but I never saw her, at least not since I can remember. They won't like it if I don't, you know; it wouldn't be very polite."

"All right," assented Tom with dignity. "I'll take you there at once: perhaps we can catch a car or something."

"I'm ashamed to ask for anything more when you've been so kind," said Nancy, after a few moments of anxious silence. "I don't know that you can think of any good chance, but I'd give a great deal if I could only go somewhere and see some pretty dancing. You know I'm always dreamin' and dreamin' about pretty dancing!" and she looked eagerly at Tom to see what he would say. "It must be goin' on somewhere in Boston," she went on with pleading eyes. "Could you ask somebody? They said at uncle Ezra's that if cousin Abby Snow wanted me to remain until to-morrow it might be just as well to stay; she used to be so well acquainted with mother. And so I thought—I might get some nice chance to look on."

"To see some dancing," repeated Tom, mindful of his own gay evening the night before, and of others to come, and the general impossibility of Nancy's finding the happiness she sought. He never had been so confronted by social barriers. As for Nancy's dancing at East Rodney, in the schoolhouse hall or in Jacob Parker's new barn, it had been one of the most ideal things he had ever known in his life; it would be hard to find elsewhere such grace as hers. In seaboard towns one often comes upon strange foreign inheritances, and the soul of a Spanish grandmother might still survive in Nancy, as far as her light feet were concerned. She danced like a flower in the wind. She made you feel light of foot yourself, as if you were whirling and blowing and waving through the air; as if you could go out dancing and dancing over the deep blue sea water of the bay, and find floor enough to touch and whirl upon. But Nancy had always seemed to take her gifts for granted; she had the simplicity of genius. "I can't say now, but I am sure to find out," said Tom Aldis definitely. "I'll try to make some sort of plan for you. I wish we could have another dance, ourselves."

"Oh, not now," answered Nancy sensibly. "It's knowing 'most all the people that makes a party pleasant."

"My aunt would have asked you to come to luncheon to-day, but she had to go out of town, and was afraid of not getting back in season. She would like to see you very much. You see, I'm only a bachelor in lodgings, this winter," explained Tom bravely.

"You've been just as good as you could be. I know all about Boston now, almost as if I lived here. I should like to see the inside of one of those big houses," she added softly; "they all look so noble as you go by. I think it was very polite of your aunt; you must thank her, Mr. Aldis."

It seemed to Tom as if his companion were building most glorious pleasure out of very commonplace materials. All the morning she had been as gay and busy as a brook.

By the middle of the afternoon he knocked again at cousin Snow's door in Revere Street, and delivered an invitation. Mrs. Annesley, his aunt, and the kindest of women, would take Nancy to an afternoon class at Papanti's, and bring her back afterwards, if cousin Snow were willing to spare her. Tom would wait and drive back with her in the coupe; then he must hurry to Cambridge for a business meeting to which he had been suddenly summoned.

Nancy was radiant when she first appeared, but a few minutes later, as they drove away together, she began to look grave and absent. It was only because she was so sorry to think of parting.

"I am so glad about the dancing class," said Tom. "I never should have thought of that. They are all children, you know; but it's very pretty, and they have all the new dances. I used to think it a horrid penance when I was a small boy."

"I don't know why it is," said Nancy, "but the mere thought of music and dancin' makes me feel happy. I never saw any real good dancin', either, but I can always think what it ought to be. There's nothing so beautiful to me as manners," she added softly, as if she whispered at the shrine of confidence.

"My aunt thinks there are going to be some pretty figure dances to-day," announced Tom in a matter-of-fact way. There was something else than the dancing upon his mind. He thought that he ought to tell Nancy of his engagement,—not that it was quite an engagement yet,—but he could not do it just now. "What was it you were going to tell me this morning? About Addie Porter, wasn't it?" He laughed a little, and then colored deeply. He had been somewhat foolish in his attentions to this young person, the beguiling village belle of East Rodney and the adjacent coasts. She was a pretty creature and a sad flirt, with none of the real beauty and quaint sisterly ways of Nancy. "What was it all about?" he asked again.

Nancy turned away quickly. "That's one thing I wanted to come to Boston for; that's what I want to tell you. She don't really care anything about you. She only wanted to get you away from the other girls. I know for certain that she likes Joe Brown better than anybody, and now she's been going with him almost all winter long. He keeps telling round that they're going to be married in the spring; but I thought if they were, she'd ask me to get some of her best things while I was in Boston. I suppose she's intendin' to play with him a while longer," said Nancy with honest scorn, "just because he loves her well enough to wait. But don't you worry about her, Mr. Aldis!"

"I won't indeed," answered Tom meekly, but with an unexpected feeling of relief as if the unconscious danger had been a real one. Nancy was very serious.

"I'm going home the first of the week," she said as they parted; but the small hand felt colder than usual, and did not return his warm grasp. The light in her eyes had all gone, but Tom's beamed affectionately.

"I never thought of Addie Porter afterward, I'm afraid," he confessed. "What awfully good fun we all had! I should like to go down to East Rodney again some time."

"Oh, shan't you ever come?" cried Nancy, with a thrill in her voice which Tom did not soon forget. He did not know that the young girl's heart was waked, he was so busy with the affairs of his own affections; but true friendship does not grow on every bush, in Boston or East Rodney, and Nancy's voice and farewell look touched something that lay very deep within his heart.

There is a little more to be told of this part of the story. Mrs. Annesley, Tom's aunt, being a woman whose knowledge of human nature and power of sympathy made her a woman of the world rather than of any smaller circle,—Mrs. Annesley was delighted with Nancy's unaffected pleasure and self-forgetful dignity of behavior at the dancing-school. She took her back to the fine house, and they had half an hour together there, and only parted because Nancy was to spend the night with cousin Snow, and another old friend of her mother's was to be asked to tea. Mrs. Annesley asked her to come to see her again, whenever she was in Boston, and Nancy gratefully promised, but she never came. "I'm all through with Boston for this time," she said, with an amused smile, at parting. "I'm what one of our neighbors calls 'all flustered up,'" and she looked eagerly in her new friend's kind eyes for sympathy. "Now that I've seen this beautiful house, and you and Mr. Aldis, and some pretty dancin', I want to go right home where I belong."

Tom Aldis meant to write to Nancy when his engagement came out, but he never did; and he meant to send a long letter to her and her mother two years later, when he and his wife were going abroad for a long time; but he had an inborn hatred of letter-writing, and let that occasion pass also, though when anything made him very sorry or very glad, he had a curious habit of thinking of these East Rodney friends. Before he went to Europe he used to send them magazines now and then, or a roll of illustrated papers; and one day, in a bookstore, he happened to see a fine French book with colored portraits of famous dancers, and sent it by express to Nancy with his best remembrances. But Tom was young and much occupied, the stream of time floated him away from the shore of Maine, not toward it, ten or fifteen years passed by, his brown hair began to grow gray, and he came back from Europe after a while to a new Boston life in which reminiscences of East Rodney seemed very remote indeed.

III

One summer afternoon there were two passengers, middle-aged men, on the small steamer James Madison, which attended the comings and goings of the great Boston steamer, and ran hither and yon on errands about Penobscot Bay. She was puffing up a long inlet toward East Rodney Landing, and the two strangers were observing the green shores with great interest. Like nearly the whole stretch of the Maine coast, there was a house on almost every point and headland; but for all this, there were great tracts of untenanted country, dark untouched forests of spruces and firs, and shady coves where there seemed to be deep water and proper moorings. The two passengers were on the watch for landings and lookouts; in short, this lovely, lonely country was being frankly appraised at its probable value for lumbering or for building-lots and its relation to the real estate market. Just now there appeared to be no citizens save crows and herons, the sun was almost down behind some high hills in the west, and the Landing was in sight not very far ahead.

"It is nearly twenty years since I came down here before," said the younger of the two men, suddenly giving the conversation a personal turn. "Just after I was out of college, at any rate. My father had bought this point of land with the islands. I think he meant to come and hunt in the autumn, and was misled by false accounts of deer and moose. He sent me down to oversee something or other; I believe he had some surveyors at work, and thought they had better be looked after; so I got my chum Carew to come along, and we found plenty of trout, and had a great time until he gave his ankle a bad sprain."

"What did you do then?" asked the elder man politely, keeping his eyes on the shore.

"I stayed by, of course; I had nothing to do in those days," answered Mr. Aldis. "It was one of those nice old-fashioned country neighborhoods where there was plenty of fun among the younger people,—sailing on moonlight nights, and haycart parties, and dances, and all sorts of things. We used to go to prayer-meeting nine or ten miles off, and sewing societies. I had hard work to get away! We made excuse of Carew's ankle joint as long as we could, but he'd been all right and going everywhere with the rest of us a fortnight before we started. We waited until there was ice alongshore, I remember."

"Daniel R. Carew, was it, of the New York Stock Exchange?" asked the listener. "He strikes you as being a very grave sort of person now; doesn't like it if he finds anybody in his chair at the club, and all that."

"I can stir him up," said Mr. Aldis confidently. "Poor old fellow, he has had a good deal of trouble, one way and another. How the Landing has grown up! Why, it's a good-sized little town!"

"I'm sorry it is so late," he added, after a long look at a farm on the shore which they were passing. "I meant to go to see the people up there," and he pointed to the old farmhouse, dark and low and firm-rooted in the long slope of half-tamed, ledgy fields. Warm thoughts of Nancy filled his heart, as if they had said good-by to each other that cold afternoon in Boston only the winter before. He had not been so eager to see any one for a long time. Such is the triumph of friendship: even love itself without friendship is the victim of chance and time.

When supper was over in the Knox House, the one centre of public entertainment in East Rodney, it was past eight o'clock, and Mr. Aldis felt like a dim copy of Rip Van Winkle, or of the gay Tom Aldis who used to know everybody, and be known of all men as the planner of gayeties. He lighted a cigar as he sat on the front piazza of the hotel, and gave himself up to reflection. There was a long line of lights in the second story of a wooden building opposite, and he was conscious of some sort of public interest and excitement.

"There is going to be a time in the hall," said the landlord, who came hospitably out to join him. "The folks are going to have a dance. The proceeds will be applied to buying a bell for the new schoolhouse. They'd be pleased if you felt like stepping over; there has been a considerable number glad to hear you thought of coming down. I ain't an East Rodney man myself, but I've often heard of your residin' here some years ago. Our folks is makin' the ice cream for the occasion," he added significantly, and Mr. Aldis nodded and smiled in acknowledgment. He had meant to go out and see the Gales, if the boat had only got in in season; but boats are unpunctual in their ways, and the James Madison had been unexpectedly signaled by one little landing and settlement after another. He remembered that a great many young people were on board when they arrived, and now they appeared again, coming along the street and disappearing at the steep stairway opposite. The lighted windows were full of heads already, and there were now and then preliminary exercises upon a violin. Mr. Aldis had grown old enough to be obliged to sit and think it over about going to a ball; the day had passed when there would have been no question; but when he had finished his cigar he crossed the street, and only stopped before the lighted store window to find a proper bank bill for the doorkeeper. Then he ran up the stairs to the hall, as if he were the Tom Aldis of old. It was an embarrassing moment as he entered the low, hot room, and the young people stared at him suspiciously; but there were also elderly people scattered about who were meekly curious and interested, and one of these got clumsily upon his feet and hastened to grasp the handsome stranger by the hand.

"Nancy heard you was coming," said Mr. Gale delightedly. "She expected I should see you here, if you was just the same kind of a man you used to be. Come let's set right down, folks is crowding in; there may be more to set than there is to dance."

"How is Nancy, isn't she coming?" asked Tom, feeling the years tumble off his shoulders.

"Well as usual, poor creatur," replied the old father, with a look of surprise. "No, no; she can't go nowhere."

At that moment the orchestra struck up a military march with so much energy that further conversation was impossible. Near them was an awkward-looking young fellow, with shoulders too broad for his height, and a general look of chunkiness and dullness. Presently he rose and crossed the room, and made a bow to his chosen partner that most courtiers might have envied. It was a bow of grace and dignity.

"Pretty well done!" said Tom Aldis aloud.

Mr. Gale was beaming with smiles, and keeping time to the music with his foot and hand. "Nancy done it," he announced proudly, speaking close to his companion's ear. "That boy give her a sight o' difficulty; he used to want to learn, but 'long at the first he'd turn red as fire if he much as met a sheep in a pastur'. The last time I see him on the floor I went home an' told her he done as well as any. You can see for yourself, now they're all a-movin'."

The fresh southerly breeze came wafting into the hall and making the lamps flare. If Tom turned his head, he could see the lights out in the bay, of vessels that had put in for the night. Old Mr. Gale was not disposed for conversation so long as the march lasted, and when it was over a frisky-looking middle-aged person accosted Mr. Aldis with the undimmed friendliness of their youth; and he took her out, as behoved him, for the Lancers quadrille. From her he learned that Nancy had been for many years a helpless invalid; and when their dance was over he returned to sit out the next one with Mr. Gale, who had recovered a little by this time from the excitement of the occasion, and was eager to talk about Nancy's troubles, but still more about her gifts and activities. After a while they adjourned to the hotel piazza in company, and the old man grew still more eloquent over a cigar. He had not changed much since Tom's residence in the family; in fact, the flight of seventeen years had made but little difference in his durable complexion or the tough frame which had been early seasoned by wind and weather.

"Yes, sir," he said, "Nancy has had it very hard, but she's the life o' the neighborhood yet. For excellent judgment I never see her equal. Why, once the board o' selec'men took trouble to meet right there in her room off the kitchen, when they had to make some responsible changes in layin' out the school deestricts. She was the best teacher they ever had, a master good teacher; fitted a boy for Bowdoin College all except his Greek, that last season before she was laid aside from sickness. She took right holt to bear it the best she could, and begun to study on what kind o' things she could do. First she used to make out to knit, a-layin' there, for the store, but her hands got crippled up with the rest of her; 't is the wust kind o' rheumatics there is. She had me go round to the neighborin' schools and say that if any of the child'n was backward an slow with their lessons to send 'em up to her. Now an' then there'd be one, an' at last she'd see to some class there wasn't time for: an' here year before last the town voted her fifty dollars a year for her services. What do you think of that?"

Aldis manifested his admiration, but he could not help wishing that he had not seemed to forget so pleasant an old acquaintance, and above all wished that he had not seemed to take part in nature's great scheme to defraud her. She had begun life with such distinct rights and possibilities.

"I tell you she was the most cut up to have to stop dancin'," said Mr. Gale gayly, "but she held right on to that, same as to other things. 'I can't dance myself,' she says, 'so I'm goin' to make other folks.' You see right before you how she's kep' her word, Mr. Aldis? What always pleased her the most, from a child, was dancin'. Folks talked to her some about letting her mind rove on them light things when she appeared to be on a dyin' bed. 'David, he danced afore the Lord,' she'd tell 'em, an' her eyes would snap so, they didn't like to say no more."

Aldis laughed, the old man himself was so cheerful.

SARAH ORNE JEWETT

"Well, sir, she made 'em keep right on with the old dancin'-school she always took such part in (I guess 't was goin', wa'n't it, that fall you stopped here?); but she sent out for all the child'n she could get and learnt 'em their manners. She can see right out into the kitchen from where she is, an' she has 'em make their bows an' take their steps till they get 'em right an' feel as good as anybody. There's boys an' girls comin' an' goin' two or three times a week in the afternoon. It don't seem to be no hardship: there ain't no such good company for young or old as Nancy."

"She'll be dreadful glad to see you," the proud father ended his praises. "Oh, she's never forgot that good time she had up to Boston. You an' all your folks couldn't have treated her no better, an' you give her her heart's desire, you did so! She's never done talkin' about that pretty dancin'-school with all them lovely little child'n, an' everybody so elegant and pretty behaved. She'd always wanted to see such a lady as your aunt was. I don't know but she's right: she always maintains that when folks has good manners an' good hearts the world is their 'n, an' she was goin' to do everything she could to keep young folks from feelin' hoggish an' left out."

Tom walked out toward the farm in the bright moonlight with Mr. Gale, and promised to call as early the next day as possible. They followed the old shore path, with the sea on one side and the pointed firs on the other, and parted where Nancy's light could be seen twinkling on the hill.

IV

It was not very cheerful to look forward to seeing a friend of one's youth crippled and disabled; beside, Tom Aldis always felt a nervous dread in being where people were ill and suffering. He thought once or twice how little compassion for Nancy these country neighbors expressed. Even her father seemed inclined to boast of her, rather than to pity the poor life that was so hindered. Business affairs and conference were appointed for that afternoon, so that by the middle of the morning he found himself walking up the yard to the Gales' side door.

There was nobody within call. Mr. Aldis tapped once or twice, and then hearing a voice he went through the narrow unpainted entry into the old kitchen, a brown, comfortable place which he well remembered.

"Oh, I'm so glad to see you," Nancy was calling from her little bedroom beyond. "Come in, come in!"

He passed the doorway, and stood with his hand on hers, which lay helpless on the blue-and-white coverlet. Nancy's young eyes, untouched by years or pain or regret, looked up at him as frankly as a child's from the pillow.

"Mother's gone down into the field to pick some peas for dinner," she said, looking and looking at Tom and smiling; but he saw at last that tears were shining, too, and making her smile all the brighter. "You see now why I couldn't write," she explained. "I kept thinking I should. I didn't want anybody else to thank you for the books. Now sit right down," she begged her guest. "Father told me all he could about last night. You danced with Addie Porter."

"I did," acknowledged Tom Aldis, and they both laughed. "We talked about old times between the figures, but it seemed to me that I remembered them better than she did."

"Addie has been through with a good deal of experience since then," explained Nancy, with a twinkle in her eyes.

"I wish I could have danced again with you," said Tom bravely, "but I saw some scholars that did you credit."

"I have to dance by proxy," said Nancy; and to this there was no reply.

Tom Aldis sat in the tiny bedroom with an aching heart. Such activity and definiteness of mind, such power of loving and hunger for life, had been pent and prisoned there so many years. Nancy had made what she could of her small world of books. There was something very uncommon in her look and way of speaking; he felt like a boy beside her, he to whom the world had given its best luxury and widest opportunity. As he looked out of the small window, he saw only a ledgy pasture where sheep were straying along the slopes among the bayberry and juniper; beyond were some balsam firs and a glimpse of the sea. It was a lovely bit of landscape, but it lacked figures, and Nancy was born to be a teacher and a lover of her kind. She had only lacked opportunity, but she was equal to meeting whatever should come. One saw it in her face.

"You don't know how many times I have thought of that cold day in Boston," said Nancy from her pillows. "Your aunt was beautiful. I never could tell you about the rest of the day with her, could I? Why, it just gave me a measure to live by. I saw right off how small some things were that I thought were big. I told her about one or two things down here in Rodney that troubled me, and she understood all about it. 'If we mean to be happy and useful,' she said, 'the only way is to be self-forgetful.' I never forgot that!"

"The seed fell upon good ground, didn't it?" said Mr. Aldis with a smile. He had been happy enough himself, but Nancy's happiness appeared in that moment to have been of another sort. He could not help thinking what a wonderful perennial quality there is in friendship. Because it had once flourished and bloomed, no winter snows of Maine could bury it, no summer sunshine of foreign life could wither this single flower of a day long past. The years vanished like a May snowdrift, and because they had known each other once they found each other now.

It was like a tough little sprig of gray everlasting; the New England edelweiss that always keeps a white flower ready to blossom safe and warm in its heart.

They entertained each other delightfully that late summer morning. Tom talked of his wife and children as he had seldom talked of them to any one before, and afterward explained the land interests which had brought him back at this late day to East Rodney.

"I came down meaning to sell my land to a speculator," he said, "or to a real estate agency which has great possessions along the coast; but I'm very doubtful about doing it, now that I have seen the bay again and this lovely shore. I had no idea that it was such a magnificent piece of country. I was going on from here to Mount Desert, with a half idea of buying land there. Why isn't this good enough that I own already? With a yacht or a good steam launch we shouldn't be so far away from places along the coast, you know. What if I were to build a house above Sunday Cove, on the headland, and if we should be neighbors! I have a friend who might build another house on the point beyond; we came home from abroad at about the same time, and he's looking for a place to build, this side of Bar Harbor." Tom was half confiding in his old acquaintance, and half thinking aloud. "These real estate brokers can't begin to give a man the value of such land as mine," he added.

"It would be excellent business to come and live here yourself, if you want to bring up the value of the property," said Nancy gravely. "I hear there are a good many lots staked out between here and Portland, but it takes more than that to start things. There can't be any prettier place than East Rodney," she declared, looking affectionately out of her little north window. "It would be a great blessing to city people, if they could come and have our good Rodney air."

The friends talked on a little longer, and with great cheerfulness and wealth of reminiscence. Tom began to understand why nobody seemed to pity Nancy, though she did at last speak sadly, and make confession that she felt it to be very hard because she never could get about the neighborhood to see any of the old and sick people. Some of them were lonesome, and lived in lonesome places. "I try to send word to them sometimes, if I can't do any more," said Nancy. "We're so apt to forget 'em, and let 'em feel they aren't useful. I can't bear to see an old heart begging for a little love. I do sometimes wish I could manage to go an' try to make a little of their time pass pleasant."

"Do you always stay just here?" asked Tom with sudden compassion, after he had stood for a moment looking out at the gray sheep on the hillside.

"Oh, sometimes I get into the old rocking-chair, and father pulls me out into the kitchen when I'm extra well," said Nancy proudly, as if she spoke of a yachting voyage or a mountaineer's exploits. "Once a doctor said if I was only up to Boston"—her voice fell a little with a touch of wistfulness—"perhaps I could have had more done, and could have got about with some kind of a chair. But that was a good while ago: I never let myself worry about it. I am so busy right here that I don't know what would happen if I set out to travel."

SARAH ORNE JEWETT

V

A year later the East Rodney shore looked as green as ever, and the untouched wall of firs and pines faithfully echoed the steamer's whistle. In the twelve months just past Mr. Aldis had worked wonders upon his long-neglected estate, and now was comfortably at housekeeping on the Sunday Cove headland. Nancy could see the chimneys and a gable of the fine establishment from her own little north window, and the sheep still fed undisturbed on the slopes that lay between. More than this, there were two other new houses, to be occupied by Tom's friends, within the distance of a mile or two. It would be difficult to give any idea of the excitement and interest of East Rodney, or the fine effect and impulse to the local market. Tom's wife and children were most affectionately befriended by their neighbors the Gales, and with their coming in midsummer many changes for the better took place in Nancy's life, and made it bright. She lost no time in starting a class, where the two eldest for the first time found study a pleasure, while little Tom was promptly and tenderly taught his best bow, and made to mind his steps with such interest and satisfaction that he who had once roared aloud in public at the infant dancing-class, now knew both confidence and ambition. There was already a well-worn little footpath between the old Gale house and Sunday Cove; it wound in and out among the ledges and thickets, and over the short sheep-turf of the knolls; and there was a scent of sweet-brier here, and of raspberries there, and of the salt water and the pines, and the juniper and bayberry, all the way.

Nancy herself had followed that path in a carrying-chair, and joy was in her heart at every step. She blessed Tom over and over again, as he walked, broad-shouldered and strong, between the forward handles, and turned his head now and then to see if she liked the journey. For many reasons, she was much better now that she could get out into the sun. The bedroom with the north window was apt to be tenantless, and where-ever Nancy went she made other people wiser and happier, and more interested in life.

On the day when she went in state to visit the new house, with her two sober carriers, and a gay little retinue of young people frisking alongside, she felt happy enough by the way; but when she got to the house itself, and had been carried quite round it, and was at last set down in the wide hall to look about, she gave her eyes a splendid liberty of enjoyment. Mrs. Aldis disappeared for a moment to give directions in her guest's behalf, and the host and Nancy were left alone together.

"No, I don't feel a bit tired," said the guest, looking pale and radiant. "I feel as if I didn't know how to be grateful enough. I have everything in the world to make me happy. What does make you and your dear family do so much?"

"It means a great deal to have friends, doesn't it?" answered Tom in a tone that thanked her warmly. "I often wish"—

He could not finish his sentence, for he was thinking of Nancy's long years, and the bond of friendship that absence and even forgetfulness had failed to break; of the curious insistence of fate which made him responsible for something in the life of Nancy and brought him back to her neighborhood. It was a moment of deep thought; he even forgot Nancy herself. He heard the water plashing on the shore below, and felt the cool sea wind that blew in at the door.

Nancy reached out her bent and twisted hand and began to speak; then she hesitated, and glanced at her hand again, and looked straight at him with shining eyes.

"There never has been a day when I haven't thought of you," she said.

FAME'S LITTLE DAY

I

Nobody ever knew, except himself, what made a foolish young newspaper reporter, who happened into a small old-fashioned hotel in New York, observe Mr. Abel Pinkham with deep interest, listen to his talk, ask a question or two of the clerk, and then go away and make up an effective personal paragraph for one of the morning papers. He must have had a heart full of fun, this young reporter, and something honestly rustic and pleasing must have struck him in the guest's demeanor, for there was a flavor in the few lines he wrote that made some of his fellows seize upon the little paragraph, and copy it, and add to it, and keep it moving. Nobody knows what starts such a thing in journalism, or keeps it alive after it is started, but on a certain Thursday morning the fact was made known to the world that among the notabilities then in the city, Abel Pinkham, Esquire, a distinguished citizen of Wetherford, Vermont, was visiting New York on important affairs connected with the maple-sugar industry of his native State. Mr. Pinkham had expected to keep his visit unannounced, but it was likely to occasion much interest in business and civic circles. This was something like the way that the paragraph started; but here and there a kindred spirit of the original journalist caught it up and added discreet lines about Mr. Pinkham's probable stay in town, his occupation of an apartment on the fourth floor of the Ethan Allen Hotel, and other circumstances so uninteresting to the reading public in general that presently in the next evening edition, one city editor after another threw out the item, and the young journalists, having had their day of pleasure, passed on to other things.

Mr. and Mrs. Pinkham had set forth from home with many forebodings, in spite of having talked all winter about taking this journey as soon as the spring opened. They would have caught at any reasonable excuse for giving it up altogether, because when the time arrived it seemed so much easier to stay at home. Mrs. Abel Pinkham had never seen New York; her husband himself had not been to the city for a great many years; in fact, his reminiscences of the former visit were not altogether pleasant, since he had foolishly fallen into many snares, and been much gulled in his character of honest young countryman. There was a tarnished and worthless counterfeit of a large gold watch still concealed between the outer boarding and inner lath and plaster of the lean-to bedroom which Mr. Abel Pinkham had occupied as a bachelor; it was not the only witness of his being taken in by city sharpers, and he had winced ever since at the thought of their wiles. But he was now a man of sixty, well-to-do, and of authority in town affairs; his children were all well married and settled in homes of their own, except a widowed daughter, who lived at home with her young son, and was her mother's lieutenant in household affairs.

The boy was almost grown, and at this season, when the maple sugar was all made and shipped, and it was still too early for spring work on the land, Mr. Pinkham could leave home as well as not, and here he was in New York, feeling himself to be a stranger and foreigner to city ways. If it had not been for that desire to appear well in his wife's eyes, which had buoyed him over the bar of many difficulties, he could have found it in his heart to take the next train back to Wetherford, Vermont, to be there rid of his best clothes and the stiff rim of his heavy felt hat. He could not let his wife discover that the noise and confusion of Broadway had the least power to make him flinch: he cared no more for it than for the woods in snow-time. He was as good as anybody, and she was better. They owed nobody a cent; and they had come on purpose to see the city of New York.

They were sitting at the breakfast-table in the Ethan Allen Hotel, having arrived at nightfall the day before. Mrs. Pinkham looked a little pale about the mouth. She had been kept awake nearly all night by the noise, and had enjoyed but little the evening she had spent in the stuffy parlor of the hotel, looking down out of the window at what seemed to her but garish scenes, and keeping a reproachful and suspicious eye upon some unpleasantly noisy young women of forward behavior who were her only companions. Abel himself was by no means so poorly entertained in the hotel office and smoking-room. He felt much more at home than she did, being better used to meeting strange men than she was to strange women, and he found two or three companions who had seen more than he of New York life. It was there, indeed, that the young reporter found him, hearty and country-fed, and loved the appearance of his best clothes, and the way Mr. Abel Pinkham brushed his hair, and loved the way that he spoke in a loud and manful voice the belief and experience of his honest heart.

In the morning at breakfast-time the Pinkhams were depressed. They missed their good bed at home; they were troubled by the roar and noise of the streets that hardly stopped over night before it began again in the morning. The waiter did not put what mind he may have had to the business of serving them; and Mrs. Abel Pinkham, whose cooking was the triumph of parish festivals at home, had her own opinion about the beefsteak. She was a woman of imagination, and now that she was fairly here, spectacles and all, it really pained her to find that the New York of her dreams, the metropolis of dignity and distinction, of wealth and elegance, did not seem to exist. These poor streets, these unlovely people, were the end of a great illusion. They did not like to meet each other's eyes, this worthy pair. The man began to put on an unbecoming air of assertion, and Mrs. Pinkham's face was full of lofty protest.

"My gracious me, Mary Ann! I am glad I happened to get the 'Tribune' this mornin'," said Mr. Pinkham, with sudden excitement. "Just you look here! I'd like well to know how they found out about our comin'!" and he handed the paper to his wife across the table. "There—there't is; right by my thumb," he insisted. "Can't you see it?" and he smiled like a boy as she finally brought her large spectacles to bear upon the important paragraph.

"I guess they think somethin' of us, if you don't think much o' them," continued Mr. Pinkham, grandly. "Oh, they know how to keep the run o' folks who are somebody to home! Draper and Fitch knew we was comin' this week: you know I sent word I was comin' to settle with them myself. I suppose they send folks round to the hotels, these newspapers, but I shouldn't thought there'd been time. Anyway, they've thought 't was worthwhile to put us in!"

Mrs. Pinkham did not take the trouble to make a mystery out of the unexpected pleasure. "I want to cut it out an' send it right up home to daughter Sarah," she said, beaming with pride, and looking at the printed names as if they were flattering photographs. "I think 't was most too strong to say we was among the notables. But there! 'tis their business to dress up things, and they have to print somethin' every day. I guess I shall go up and put on my best dress," she added, inconsequently; "this one's kind of dusty; it's the same I rode in."

"Le' me see that paper again," said Mr. Pinkham jealously. "I didn't more 'n half sense it, I was so taken aback. Well, Mary Ann, you didn't expect you was goin' to get into the papers when you came away. *Abel Pinkham, Esquire, of Wetherford, Vermont.*' It looks well, don't it? But you might have knocked me down with a feather when I first caught sight of them words."

"I guess I shall put on my other dress," said Mrs. Pinkham, rising, with quite a different air from that with which she had sat down to her morning meal. "This one looks a little out o' style, as Sarah said, but when I got up this mornin' I was so homesick it didn't seem to make any kind o' difference. I expect that saucy girl last night took us to be nobodies. I'd like to leave the paper round where she couldn't help seein' it."

"Don't take any notice of her," said Abel, in a dignified tone. "If she can't do what you want an' be civil, we'll go somewheres else. I wish I'd done what we talked of at first an' gone to the Astor House, but that young man in the cars told me 't was remote from the things we should want to see. The Astor House was the top o' everything when I was here last, but I expected to find some changes. I want you to have the best there is," he said, smiling at his wife as if they were just making their wedding journey. "Come, let's be stirrin'; 't is long past eight o'clock," and he ushered her to the door, newspaper in hand.

II

L ater that day the guests walked up Broadway, holding themselves erect, and feeling as if every eye was upon them. Abel Pinkham had settled with his correspondents for the spring consignments of maple sugar, and a round sum in bank bills was stowed away in his breast pocket. One of the partners had been a Wetherford boy, so when there came a renewal of interest in maple sugar, and the best confectioners were ready to do it honor, the finest quality being at a large premium, this partner remembered that there never was any sugar made in Wetherford of such melting and delicious flavor as from the trees on the old Pinkham farm. He had now made a good bit of money for himself on this private venture, and was ready that morning to pay Mr. Abel Pinkham cash down, and to give him a handsome order for the next season for all he could make. Mr. Fitch was also generous in the matter of such details as freight and packing; he was immensely polite and kind to his old friends, and begged them to come out and stay with him and his wife, where they lived now, in a not far distant New Jersey town.

"No, no, sir," said Mr. Pinkham promptly. "My wife has come to see the city, and our time is short. Your folks'll be up this summer, won't they? We'll wait an' visit then."

"You must certainly take Mrs. Pinkham up to the Park," said the commission merchant. "I wish I had time to show you round myself. I suppose you've been seeing some things already, haven't you? I noticed your arrival in the 'Herald.'"

"The 'Tribune' it was," said Mr. Pinkham, blushing through a smile and looking round at his wife.

"Oh no; I never read the 'Tribune,'" said Mr. Fitch. "There was quite an extended notice in my paper. They must have put you and Mrs. Pinkham into the 'Herald' too." And so the friends parted, laughing. "I am much pleased to have a call from such distinguished parties," said Mr. Fitch, by way of final farewell, and Mr. Pinkham waved his hand grandly in reply.

"Let's get the 'Herald,' then," he said, as they started up the street. "We can go an' sit over in that little square that we passed as we came along, and rest an' talk things over about what we'd better do this afternoon. I'm tired out a-trampin' and standin'. I'd rather have set still while we were there, but he wanted us to see his store. Done very well, Joe Fitch has, but 't ain't a business I should like."

There was a lofty look and sense of behavior about Mr. Pinkham of Wetherford. You might have thought him a great politician as he marched up Broadway, looking neither to right hand nor left. He felt himself to be a person of great responsibilities.

"I begin to feel sort of at home myself," said his wife, who always had a certain touch of simple dignity about her. "When we was comin' yesterday New York seemed to be all strange, and there wasn't nobody expectin' us. I feel now just as if I'd been here before."

They were now on the edge of the better-looking part of the town; it was still noisy and crowded, but noisy with fine carriages instead of drays, and crowded with well-dressed people. The hours for shopping and visiting were beginning, and more than one person looked with appreciative and friendly eyes at the comfortable pleased-looking elderly man and woman who went their easily beguiled and loitering way. The pavement peddlers detained them, but the cabmen beckoned them in vain; their eyes were busy with the immediate foreground. Mrs. Pinkham was embarrassed by the recurring reflection of herself in the great windows.

"I wish I had seen about a new bonnet before we came," she lamented. "They seem to be havin' on some o' their spring things."

"Don't you worry, Mary Ann. I don't see anybody that looks any better than you do," said Abel, with boyish and reassuring pride.

Mr. Pinkham had now bought the "Herald," and also the "Sun," well recommended by an able newsboy, and presently they crossed over from that corner by the Fifth Avenue Hotel which seems like the very heart of New York, and found a place to sit down on the Square—an empty bench, where they could sit side by side and look the papers through, reading over each other's shoulder, and being impatient from page to page. The paragraph was indeed repeated, with trifling additions. Ederton of the "Sun" had followed the "Tribune" man's lead, and fabricated a brief interview, a marvel of art and discretion, but so general in its allusions that it could create no suspicion; it almost deceived Mr. Pinkham himself, so that he found unaffected pleasure in the fictitious occasion, and felt as if he had easily covered himself with glory. Except for the bare fact of the interview's being imaginary, there was no discredit to be cast upon Mr. Abel Pinkham's having said that he thought the country near Wetherford looked well for the time of year, and promised a fair hay crop, and that his income was augmented one half to three fifths by his belief in the future of maple sugar. It was likely to be the great coming crop of the Green Mountain State. Ederton suggested that there was talk of Mr. Pinkham's presence in the matter of a great maple-sugar trust, in which much of the capital of Wall Street would be involved.

"How they do hatch up these things, don't they?" said the worthy man at this point. "Well, it all sounds well, Mary Ann."

"It says here that you are a very personable man," smiled his wife, "and have filled some of the most responsible town offices" (this was the turn taken by Goffey of the "Herald"). "Oh, and that you are going to attend the performance at Barnum's this evening, and occupy reserved seats. Why, I didn't know—who have you told about that?—who was you talkin' to last night, Abel?"

"I never spoke o' goin' to Barnum's to any livin' soul," insisted Abel, flushing. "I only thought of it two or three times to myself that perhaps I might go an' take you. Now that is singular; perhaps they put that in just to advertise the show."

"Ain't it a kind of a low place for folks like us to be seen in?" suggested Mrs. Pinkham timidly. "People seem to be payin' us all this attention, an' I don't know's 't would be dignified for us to go to one o' them circus places."

"I don't care; we shan't live but once. I ain't comin' to New York an' confine myself to evenin' meetin's," answered Abel, throwing away discretion and morality together. "I tell you I'm goin' to spend this sugar-money just as we've a mind to. You've worked hard, an' counted a good while on comin', and so've I; an' I ain't goin' to mince my steps an' pinch an' screw for nobody. I'm goin' to hire one o' them hacks an' ride up to the Park."

"Joe Fitch said we could go right up in one o' the elevated railroads for five cents, an' return when we was ready," protested Mary Ann, who had a thriftier inclination than her husband; but Mr. Pinkham was not to be let or hindered, and they presently found themselves going up Fifth Avenue in a somewhat battered open landau. The spring sun shone upon them, and the spring breeze fluttered the black ostrich tip on Mrs. Pinkham' s durable winter bonnet, and brought the pretty color to her faded cheeks.

"There! this is something like. Such people as we are can't go meechin' round; it ain't expected. Don't it pay for a lot o' hard work?" said Abel; and his wife gave him a pleased look for her only answer. They were both thinking of their gray farmhouse high on a long western slope, with the afternoon sun full in its face, the old red barn, the pasture, the shaggy woods that stretched far up the mountain-side.

"I wish Sarah an' little Abel was here to see us ride by," said Mary Ann Pinkham, presently. "I can't seem to wait to have 'em get that newspaper. I'm so glad we sent it right off before we started this mornin'. If Abel goes to the post-office comin' from school, as he always does, they'll have it to read to-morrow before supper-time."

III

This happy day in two plain lives ended, as might have been expected, with the great Barnum show. Mr. and Mrs. Pinkham found themselves in possession of countless advertising cards and circulars next morning, and these added somewhat to their sense of responsibility. Mrs. Pinkham became afraid that the hotel-keeper would charge them double. "We've got to pay for it some way; there. I don't know but I'm more 'n willin'," said the good soul. "I never did have such a splendid time in all my life. Findin' you so respected 'way off here is the best of anything; an' then seein' them dear little babies in their nice carriages, all along the streets and up to the Central Park! I never shall forget them beautiful little creatur's. And then the houses, an' the hosses, an' the store windows, an' all the rest of it! Well, I can't make my country pitcher hold no more, an' I want to get home an' think it over, goin' about my housework."

They were just entering the door of the Ethan Allen Hotel for the last time, when a young man met them and bowed cordially. He was the original reporter of their arrival, but they did not know it, and the impulse was strong within him to formally invite Mr. Pinkham to make an address before the members of the Produce Exchange on the following morning; but he had been a country boy himself, and their look of seriousness and self-consciousness appealed to him unexpectedly. He wondered what effect this great experience would have upon their after-life. The best fun, after all, would be to send marked copies of his paper and Ederton's to all the weekly newspapers in that part of Vermont. He saw before him the evidence of their happy increase of self-respect, and he would make all their neighborhood agree to do them honor. Such is the dominion of the press.

"Who was that young man?—he kind of bowed to you," asked the lady from Wetherford, after the journalist had meekly passed; but Abel Pinkham, Esquire, could only tell her that he looked like a young fellow who was sitting in the office the evening that they came to the hotel. The reporter did not seem to these distinguished persons to be a young man of any consequence.

A WAR DEBT

I

There was a tinge of autumn color on even the English elms as Tom Burton walked slowly up Beacon Street. He was wondering all the way what he had better do with himself; it was far too early to settle down in Boston for the winter, but his grandmother kept to her old date for moving up to town, and here they were. As yet nobody thought of braving the country weather long after October came in, and most country houses were poorly equipped with fireplaces, or even furnaces: this was some years ago, and not the very last autumn that ever was.

There was likely to be a long stretch of good weather, a month at least, if one took the trouble to go a little way to the southward. Tom Burton quickened his steps a little, and began to think definitely of his guns, while a sudden resolve took shape in his mind. Just then he reached the doorsteps of his grandmother's fine old-fashioned house, being himself the fourth Thomas Burton that the shining brass door-plate had represented. His old grandmother was the only near relative he had in the world; she was growing older and more dependent upon him every day. That summer he had returned from a long wandering absence of three years, and the vigorous elderly woman whom he had left, busy and self-reliant, had sadly changed in the mean time; age had begun to strike telling blows at her strength and spirits. Tom had no idea of leaving her again for the long journeys which had become the delightful habit of his life; but there was no reason why he should not take a fortnight's holiday now and then, particularly now.

"Has Mrs. Burton come down yet, Dennis? Is there any one with her?" asked Tom, as he entered.

"There is not, sir. Mrs. Burton is in the drawing-room," answered Dennis precisely. "The tea is just going up; I think she was waiting for you." And Tom ran upstairs like a schoolboy, and then walked discreetly into the drawing-room. His grandmother gave no sign of having expected him, but she always liked company at that hour of the day: there had come to be too many ghosts in the empty chairs.

"Can I have two cups?" demanded the grandson, cheerfully. "I don't know when I have had such a walk!" and they began a gay gossiping hour together, and parted for a short season afterward, only to meet again at dinner, with a warm sense of pleasure in each other's company. The young man always insisted that his grandmother was the most charming woman in the world, and it can be imagined what the grandmother thought of Tom. She was only severe with him because he had given no signs of wishing to marry, but she was tolerant of all delay, so long as she could now and then keep the subject fresh in his mind. It was not a moment to speak again of the great question that afternoon, and she had sat and listened to his talk of people and things, a little plaintive and pale, but very handsome, behind the tea-table.

II

At dinner, after Dennis had given Tom his cup of coffee and cigars, and disappeared with an accustomed air of thoughtfully leaving the family alone for a private interview, Mrs. Burton, who sometimes lingered if she felt like talking, and sometimes went away to the drawing-room to take a brief nap before she began her evening book, and before Tom joined her for a few minutes to say good-night if he were going out,—Mrs. Burton left her chair more hurriedly than usual. Tom meant to be at home that evening, and was all ready to speak of his plan for some Southern shooting, and he felt a sudden sense of disappointment.

"Don't go away," he said, looking up as she passed. "Is this a bad cigar?"

"No, no, my dear," said the old lady, hurrying across the room in an excited, unusual sort of way. "I wish to show you something while we are by ourselves." And she stooped to unlock a little cupboard in the great sideboard, and fumbled in the depths there, upsetting and clanking among some pieces of silver. Tom joined her with a pair of candles, but it was some moments before she could find what she wanted. Mrs. Burton appeared to be in a hurry, which almost never happened, and in trying to help her Tom dropped much wax unheeded at her side.

"Here it is at last," she said, and went back to her seat at the table. "I ought to tell you the stories of some old silver that I keep in that cupboard; if I were to die, nobody would know anything about them."

"Do you mean the old French spoons, and the prince's porringer, and those things?" asked Tom, showing the most lively interest. But his grandmother was busy unfastening the strings of a little bag, and shook her head absently in answer to his question. She took out and handed to him a quaint old silver cup with two handles, that he could not remember ever to have seen.

"What a charming old bit!" said he, turning it about. "Where in the world did it come from? English, of course; and it looks like a loving-cup. A copy of some old Oxford thing, perhaps; only they didn't copy much then. I should think it had been made for a child." Tom turned it round and round and drew the candles toward him. "Here's an inscription, too, but very much worn."

"Put it down a minute," said Mrs. Burton impatiently. "Every time I have thought of it I have been more and more ashamed to have it in the house. People weren't so shocked by such things at first; they would only be sentimental about the ruined homes, and say that, 'after all, it was the fortune of war.' That cup was stolen."

"But who stole it?" inquired Tom, with deep interest.

"Your father brought it here," said Mrs. Burton, with great spirit, and even a tone of reproach. "My son, Tom Burton, your father, brought it home from the war. I think his plan was to keep it safe to send back to the owners. But he left it with your mother when he was ordered suddenly to the front; he was only at home four days, and the day after he got back to camp was the day he was killed, poor boy"—

"I remember something about it now," Tom hastened to say. "I remember my mother's talking about the breaking up of Southern homes, and all that; she never believed it until she saw the cup, and I thought it was awfully silly. I was at the age when I could have blown our own house to pieces just for the sake of the racket."

"And that terrible year your grandfather's and your mother's death followed, and I was left alone with you—two of us out of the five that had made my home"—

"I should say one and a half," insisted Tom, with some effort. "What a boy I was for a grandson! Thank Heaven, there comes a time when we are all the same age! We are jolly together now, aren't we? Come, dear old lady, don't let's think too much of what's gone by;" and he went round the table and gave her a kiss, and stood there where she need not look him in the face, holding her dear thin hand as long as ever she liked.

"I want you to take that silver cup back, Tom," she said presently, in her usual tone. "Go back and finish your coffee." She had seldom broken down like this. Mrs. Burton had been self-possessed, even to apparent coldness, in earlier life.

"How in the world am I going to take it back?" asked Tom, most businesslike and calm. "Do you really know just where it came from? And then it was several years ago."

"Your grandfather knew; they were Virginia people, of course, and happened to be old friends; one of the younger men was his own classmate. He knew the crest and motto at once, but there were two or three branches of the family, none of them, so far as he knew, living anywhere near where your father was in camp. Poor Tom said that there

SARAH ORNE JEWETT

was a beautiful old house sacked and burnt, and everything scattered that was saved. He happened to hear a soldier from another regiment talking about it, and saw him tossing this cup about, and bought it from him with all the money he happened to have in his pockets."

"Then he didn't really steal it himself!" exclaimed Tom, laughing a little, and with a sense of relief.

"No, no, Tom!" said Mrs. Burton impatiently. "Only you see that it really is a stolen thing, and I have had it all this time under my roof. For a long time it was packed away with your father's war relics, those things that I couldn't bear to see. And then I would think of it only at night after I had once seen it, and forget to ask any one else while you were away, or wait for you to come. Oh, I have no excuse. I have been very careless, but here it has been all the time. I wish you would find out about the people; there must be some one belonging to them—some friend, perhaps, to whom we could give it. This is one of the things that I wish to have done, and to forget. Just take it back, or write some letters first: you will know what to do. I should like to have the people understand."

"I'll see about it at once," said Tom, with great zest. "I believe you couldn't have spoken at a better time. I have been thinking of going down to Virginia this very week. I hear that they are in a hurry with fitting out that new scientific expedition in Washington that I declined to join, and they want me to come on and talk over things before they are off. One of the men is a Virginian, an awfully good fellow; and then there's Clendennin, my old chum, who's in Washington, too, just now; they'll give me my directions; they know all Virginia between them. I'll take the cup along, and run down from Washington for a few days, and perhaps get some shooting."

Tom's face was shining with interest and satisfaction; he took the cup and again held it under the candle-light. "How pretty this old chasing is round the edge, and the set of the little handles! Oh, here's the motto! What a dear old thing, and enormously old! See here, under the crest," and he held it toward Mrs. Burton:—

"Je vous en prie Bel-ami."

Mrs. Burton glanced at it with indifference. "Yes, it is charming, as you say. But I only wish to return it to its owners, Tom."

"Je vous en prie Bel-ami."

Tom repeated the words under his breath, and looked at the crest carefully.

"I remember that your grandfather said it belonged to the Bellamys," said his grandmother. "Of course: how could I forget that? I have never looked at it properly since the day I first saw it. It is a charming motto— they were very charming and distinguished people. I suppose this is a pretty way of saying that they could not live without their friends. I beg of you, Belami;—it is a quaint fancy; one might turn it in two or three pretty ways."

"Or they may have meant that they only looked to themselves for what they wanted, *Je vous en prie Bellamy!*" said Tom gallantly. "All right; I think that I shall start to-morrow or next day. If you have no special plans," he added.

"Do go, my dear; you may get some shooting, as you say," said Mrs. Burton, a little wistfully, but kindly personifying Tom's inclination.

"You've started me off on a fine romantic adventure," said the young man, smiling. "Come; my cigar's gone out, and it never was good for much; let's go in and try the cards, and talk about things; perhaps you'll think of something more about the Bellamys. You said that my grandfather had a classmate"—

Mrs. Burton stopped to put the cup into its chamois bag again, and handed it solemnly to Tom, then she took his arm, and dismissing all unpleasant thoughts, they sat down to the peaceful game of cribbage to while away the time. The grandson lent himself gayly to pleasure-making, and they were just changing the cards for their books, when one of the elder friends of the house appeared, one of the two or three left who called Mrs. Burton Margaret, and was greeted affectionately as Henry in return. This guest always made the dear lady feel young; he himself was always to the front of things, and had much to say. It was quite forgotten that a last charge had been given to Tom, or that the past had been wept over. Presently, the late evening hours being always her best, she forgot in eager talk that she had any grandson at all, and Tom slipped away with his book to his own sitting-room and his pipe. He took the little cup out of its bag again, and set it before him, and began to lay plans for a Southern journey.

III

The Virginia country was full of golden autumn sunshine and blue haze. The long hours spent on a slow-moving train were full of shocks and surprises to a young traveler who knew almost every civilized country better than his own. The lonely look of the fields, the trees shattered by war, which had not yet had time enough to muffle their broken tops with green; the negroes, who crowded on board the train, lawless, and unequal to holding their liberty with steady hands, looked poor and less respectable than in the old plantation days—it was as if the long discipline of their former state had counted for nothing. Tom Burton felt himself for the first time to have something of a statesman's thoughts and schemes as he moralized along the way. Presently he noticed with deep sympathy a lady who came down the crowded car, and took the seat just in front of him. She carried a magazine under her arm a copy of—"Blackwood," which was presently proved to bear the date of 1851, and to be open at an article on the death of Wordsworth. She was the first lady he had seen that day—there was little money left for journeying and pleasure among the white Virginians; but two or three stations beyond this a group of young English men and women stood with the gay negroes on the platform, and came into the train with cheerful greetings to their friends. It seemed as if England had begun to settle Virginia all over again, and their clear, lively voices had no foreign sound. There were going to be races at some court-house town in the neighborhood. Burton was a great lover of horses himself, and the new scenes grew more and more interesting. In one of the gay groups was a different figure from any of the fresh-cheeked young wives of the English planters—a slender girl, pale and spirited, with a look of care beyond her years. She was the queen of her little company. It was to her that every one looked for approval and sympathy as the laugh went to and fro. There was something so high-bred and elegant in her bearing, something so exquisitely sure and stately, that her companions were made clumsy and rustic in their looks by contrast. The eager talk of the coming races, of the untried thoroughbreds, the winners and losers of the year before, made more distinct this young Virginia lady's own look of high-breeding, and emphasized her advantage of race. She was the newer and finer Norman among Saxons. She alone seemed to have that inheritance of swiftness of mind, of sureness of training. It was the highest type of English civilization refined still further by long growth in favoring soil. Tom Burton read her unconscious face as if it were a romance; he believed that one of the great Virginia houses must still exist, and that she was its young mistress. The house's fortune was no doubt gone; the long-worn and carefully mended black silk gown that followed the lines of her lovely figure told plainly enough that worldly prosperity was a thing of the past. But what nature could give of its best, and only age and death could take away, were hers. He watched her more and more; at one moment she glanced up suddenly and held his eyes with hers for one revealing moment. There was no surprise in the look, but a confession of pathos, a recognition of sympathy, which made even a stranger feel that he had the inmost secret of her heart.

IV

The next day our hero, having hired a capital saddle-horse, a little the worse for age, was finding his way eastward along the sandy roads. The country was full of color; the sassafras and gum trees and oaks were all ablaze with red and yellow. Now and then he caught a glimpse of a sail on one of the wide reaches of the river which lay to the northward; now and then he passed a broken gateway or the ruins of a cabin. He carried a light gun before him across the saddle, and a game-bag hung slack and empty at his shoulder except for a single plump partridge in one corner, which had whirred up at the right moment out of a vine-covered thicket. Something small and heavy in his coat pocket seemed to correspond to the bird, and once or twice he unconsciously lifted it in the hollow of his hand. The day itself, and a sense of being on the road to fulfill his mission, a sense of unending leisure and satisfaction under that lovely hazy sky, seemed to leave no place for impatience or thought of other things. He rode slowly along, with his eye on the roadside coverts, letting the horse take his own gait, except when a ragged negro boy, on an unwilling, heavy-footed mule, slyly approached and struck the dallying steed from behind. It was past the middle of the October afternoon.

"Mos' thar now, Cun'l," said the boy at last, eagerly. "See them busted trees pas' thar, an' chimblies? You tu'n down nax' turn; ride smart piece yet, an' you come right front of ol' Mars Bell'my's house. See, he comin' 'long de road now. Yas, 'tis Mars Bell'my shore, an' 's gun."

Tom had been looking across the neglected fields with compassion, and wondering if such a plantation could ever be brought back to its days of prosperity. As the boy spoke he saw the tall chimneys in the distance, and then, a little way before him in the shadow of some trees, a stately figure that slowly approached. He hurriedly dismounted, leading his horse until he met the tall old man, who answered his salutation with much dignity. There was something royal and remote from ordinary men in his silence after the first words of courteous speech.

"Yas, sir; that's Mars Bell'my, sir," whispered the boy on the mule, reassuringly, and the moment of hesitation was happily ended.

"I was on my way to call upon you, Colonel Bellamy; my name is Burton," said the younger man.

"Will you come with me to the house?" said the old gentleman, putting out his hand cordially a second time; and though he had frowned slightly at first at the unmistakable Northern accent, the light came quickly to his eyes. Tom gave his horse's bridle to the boy, who promptly transferred himself to the better saddle, and began to lead the mule instead.

"I have been charged with an errand of friendship," said Tom. "I believe that you and my grandfather were at Harvard together." Tom looked boyish and eager and responsive to hospitality at this moment. He was straight and trim, like a Frenchman. Colonel Bellamy was much the taller of the two, even with his bent shoulders and relaxed figure.

"I see the resemblance to your grandfather, sir. I bid you welcome to Fairford," said the Colonel. "Your visit is a great kindness."

They walked on together, speaking ceremoniously of the season and of the shooting and Tom's journey, until they left the woods and overgrown avenue at the edge of what had once been a fine lawn, with clusters of huge oaks; but these were shattered by war and more or less ruined. The lopped trunks still showed the marks of fire and shot; some had put out a fresh bough or two, but most of the ancient trees stood for their own monuments, rain-bleached and gaunt. At the other side of the wide lawn, against young woodland and a glimpse of the river, were the four great chimneys which had been seen from the highroad. There was no dwelling in sight at the moment, and Tom stole an apprehensive look at the grave face of his companion. It appeared as if he were being led to the habitation of ghosts, as if he were purposely to be confronted with the desolation left in the track of Northern troops. It was not so long since the great war that these things could be forgotten.

The Colonel, however, without noticing the ruins in any way, turned toward the right as he neared them, and passing a high fragment of brick wall topped by a marble ball or two—which had been shot at for marks—and passing, just beyond, some huge clumps of box, they came to a square brick building with a rude wooden addition at one side, and saw some tumble-down sheds a short distance beyond this, with a negro cabin.

They came to the open door. "This was formerly the billiard-room. Your grandfather would have kept many memories of it," said the host simply. "Will you go in, Mr. Burton?" And Tom climbed two or three perilous wooden steps and entered, to find himself in a most homelike and charming place. There was a huge fireplace opposite the door, with a thin whiff of blue smoke going up, a few old books on the high chimney-piece, a pair of fine portraits with damaged frames, some

SARAH ORNE JEWETT

old tables and chairs of different patterns, with a couch by the square window covered with a piece of fine tapestry folded together and still showing its beauty, however raveled and worn. By the opposite window, curtained only by vines, sat a lady with her head muffled in lace, who greeted the guest pleasantly, and begged pardon for not rising from her chair. Her face wore an unmistakable look of pain and sorrow. As Tom Burton stood at her side, he could find nothing to say in answer to her apologies. He was not wont to be abashed, and a real court could not affect him like this ideal one. The poor surroundings could only be seen through the glamour of their owner's presence—it seemed a most elegant interior.

"I am sorry to have the inconvenience of deafness," said Madam Bellamy, looking up with an anxious little smile. "Will you tell me again the name of our guest?"

"He is my old classmate Burton's grandson, of Boston," said the Colonel, who now stood close at her side; he looked apprehensive as he spoke, and the same shadow flitted over his face as when Tom had announced himself by the oak at the roadside.

"I remember Mr. Burton, your grandfather, very well," said Madam Bellamy at last, giving Tom her hand for the second time, as her husband had done. "He was your guest here the autumn before we were married, my dear; a fine rider, I remember, and a charming gentleman. He was much entertained by one of our hunts. I saw that you also carried a gun. My dear," and she turned to her husband anxiously, "did you bring home any birds?"

Colonel Bellamy's face lengthened. "I had scarcely time, or perhaps I had not my usual good fortune," said he. "The birds have followed the grain-fields away from Virginia, we sometimes think."

"I can offer you a partridge," said Tom eagerly. "I shot one as I rode along. I am afraid that I stopped Colonel Bellamy just as he was going out."

"I thank you very much," said Madam Bellamy. "And you will take supper with us, certainly. You will give us the pleasure of a visit? I regret very much my granddaughter's absence, but it permits me to offer you her room, which happens to be vacant." But Tom attempted to make excuse. "No, no," said Madam Bellamy, answering her own thoughts rather than his words. "You must certainly stay the night with us; we shall make you most welcome. It will give my husband great pleasure; he will have many questions to ask you."

Tom went out to search for his attendant, who presently clattered away on the mule at an excellent homeward pace. An old negro man servant led away the horse, and Colonel Bellamy disappeared also, leaving the young guest to entertain himself and his hostess for an hour, that flew by like light. A woman who is charming in youth is still more charming in age to a man of Tom Burton's imagination, and he was touched to find how quickly the first sense of receiving an antagonist had given way before a desire to show their feeling of kindly hospitality toward a guest. The links of ancient friendship still held strong, and as Tom sat with his hostess by the window they had much pleasant talk of Northern families known to them both, of whom, or of whose children and grandchildren, he could give much news. It seemed as if he should have known Madam Bellamy all his life. It is impossible to say how she illumined her poor habitation, with what dignity and sweetness she avoided, as far as possible, any reference to the war or its effects. One could hardly remember that she was poor, or ill, or had suffered such piteous loss of friends and fortune.

Later, when Tom was walking toward the river through the woods and overgrown fields of the plantation, he came upon the ruins of the old cabins of what must have been a great family of slaves. The crumbling heaps of the chimneys stood in long lines on either side of a weed-grown lane; not far beyond he found the sinking mounds of some breastworks on a knoll which commanded the river channel. The very trees and grass looked harrowed and distressed by war; the silence of the sunset was only broken by the cry of a little owl that was begging mercy of its fears far down the lonely shore.

V

At supper that night Burton came from his room to find Colonel Bellamy bringing his wife in his arms to the table, while the old bent-backed and gray-headed man servant followed to place her chair. The mistress of Fairford was entirely lame and helpless, but she sat at the head of her table like a queen. There was a bunch of damask-roses at her plate. The Colonel himself was in evening dress, antique in cut, and sadly worn, and Tom heartily thanked his patron saint that the boy had brought his portmanteau in good season. There was a glorious light in the room from the fire, and the table was served with exquisite care, and even more luxurious delay, the excellent fish which the Colonel himself must have caught in his unexplained absence, and Tom's own partridge, which was carved as if it had been the first wild turkey of the season, were followed by a few peaches touched with splendid color as they lay on a handful of leaves in a bent and dented pewter plate. There seemed to be no use for the stray glasses, until old Milton produced a single small bottle of beer, and uncorked and poured it for his master and his master's guest with a grand air. The Colonel lifted his eyebrows slightly, but accepted its appearance at the proper moment.

They sat long at table. It was impossible to let one's thought dwell upon any of the meagre furnishings of the feast. The host and hostess talked of the days when they went often to France and England, and of Tom's grandfather when he was young. At last Madam Bellamy left the table, and Tom stood waiting while she was carried to her own room. He had kissed her hand like a courtier as he said good-night. On the Colonel's return the old butler ostentatiously placed the solitary bottle between them and went away. The Colonel offered some excellent tobacco, and Tom begged leave to fetch his pipe. When he returned he brought with it the chamois-skin bag that held the silver cup, and laid it before him on the table. It was like the dread of going into battle, but the moment had arrived. He laid his hand on the cup for a moment as if to hide it, then he waited until his pipe was fairly going.

"This is something which I have come to restore to you, sir," said Tom presently, taking the piece of silver from its wrappings. "I believe that it is your property."

The old Colonel's face wore a strange, alarmed look; his thin cheeks grew crimson. He reached eagerly for the cup, and held it before his eyes. At last he bent his head and kissed it. Tom Burton saw that his tears began to fall, that he half rose, turning toward the door of the next room, where his wife was; then he sank back again, and looked at his guest appealingly.

"I ask no questions," he faltered; "it was the fortune of war. This cup was my grandfather's, my father's, and mine; all my own children drank from it in turn; they are all gone before me. We always called it our lucky cup. I fear that it has come back too late"—The old man's voice broke, but he still held the shining piece of silver before him, and turned it about in the candle-light.

"Je vous en prie Bel-ami."

he whispered under his breath, and put the cup before him on the scarred mahogany.

VI

S hall we move our chairs before the fire, Mr. Burton? My dear wife is but frail," said the old man, after a long silence, and with touching pathos. "She sees me companioned for the evening, and is glad to seek her room early; if you were not here she would insist upon our game of cards. I do not allow myself to dwell upon the past, and I have no wish for gay company;" he added, in a lower voice, "My daily dread in life is to be separated from her."

As the evening wore on, the autumn air grew chilly, and again and again the host replenished his draughty fireplace, and pushed the box of delicious tobacco toward his guest, and Burton in his turn ventured to remember a flask in his portmanteau, and begged the Colonel to taste it, because it had been filled from an old cask in his grandfather's cellar. The butler's eyes shone with satisfaction when he was unexpectedly called upon to brew a little punch after the old Fairford fashion, and the later talk ranged along the youthful escapades of Thomas Burton the elder to the beauties and the style of Addison; from the latest improvement in shot-guns to the statesmanship of Thomas Jefferson, while the Colonel spoke tolerantly, in passing, of some slight misapprehensions of Virginia life made by a delightful young writer, too early lost—Mr. Thackeray.

Tom Burton had never enjoyed an evening more; the romance, the pathos of it, as he found himself more and more taking his grandfather's place in the mind of this hereditary friend, waked all his sympathy. The charming talk that never dwelt too long or was hurried too fast, the exquisite faded beauty of Madam Bellamy, the noble dignity and manliness of the old planter and soldier, the perfect absence of reproach for others or whining pity for themselves, made the knowledge of their regret and loss doubly poignant. Their four sons had all laid down their lives in what they believed from their hearts to be their country's service; their daughters had died early, one from sorrow at her husband's death, and one from exposure in a forced flight across country; their ancestral home lay in ruins; their beloved cause had been put to shame and defeat—yet they could bow their heads to every blast of misfortune, and could make a man welcome at their table whose every instinct and tradition of loyalty made him their enemy. The owls might shriek from the chimneys of Fairford, and the timid wild hares course up and down the weed-grown avenues on an autumn night like this, but a welcome from the Bellamys was a welcome still. It seemed to the young imaginative guest that the old motto of the house was never so full of significance as when he fancied it exchanged between the Colonel and himself, Southerner and Northerner, elder and younger man, conquered and conqueror in an unhappy war. The two old portraits, with their warped frames and bullet-holes, faded and gleamed again in the firelight; the portrait of an elderly man was like the Colonel himself, but the woman, who was younger, and who seemed to meet Tom's eye gayly enough, bore a resemblance which he could only half recall. It was very late when the two men said good-night. They were each conscious of the great delight of having found a friend. The candles had flickered out long before, but the fire still burned, and struck a ray of light from the cup on the table.

VII

The next morning Burton waked early in his tiny sleeping-room. The fragrance of ripe grapes and the autumn air blew in at the window, and he hastened to dress, especially as he could hear the footstep and imperious voice of Colonel Bellamy, who seemed to begin his new day with zest and courage in the outer room. Milton, the old gray-headed negro, was there too, and was alternately upbraided and spoken with most intimately and with friendly approval. It sounded for a time as if some great excitement and project were on foot; but Milton presently appeared, eager for morning offices, and when Tom went out to join the Colonel he was no longer there. There were no signs of breakfast. The birds were singing in the trees outside, and the sun shone in through the wide-opened door. It was a poor place in the morning light. As he crossed the room he saw an old-fashioned gift-book lying on the couch, as if some one had just laid it there face downward. He carried it with him to the door; a dull collection enough, from forgotten writers of forgotten prose and verse, but the Colonel had left it open at some lines which, with all their faults, could not be read without sympathy. He was always thinking of his wife; he had marked the four verses because they spoke of her.

Tom put the old book down just as Colonel Bellamy passed outside, and hastened to join him. They met with pleasure, and stood together talking. The elder man presently quoted a line or two of poetry about the beauty of the autumn morning, and his companion stood listening with respectful attention, but he observed by contrast the hard, warriorlike lines of the Colonel's face. He could well believe that, until sorrow had softened him, a fiery impatient temper had ruled this Southern heart. There was a sudden chatter and noise of voices, and they both turned to see a group of negroes, small and great, coming across the lawn with bags and baskets, and after a few muttered words the old master set forth hurriedly to meet them, Tom following.

"Be still, all of you!" said the Colonel sternly. "Your mistress is still asleep. Go round to Milton, and he will attend to you. I'll come presently."

They were almost all old people, many of them were already infirm, and it was hard to still their requests and complaints. One of the smaller children clasped Colonel Bellamy about the knees. There was something patriarchal in the scene, and one could not help being sure that some reason for the present poverty of Fairford was the necessity for protecting these poor souls. The merry, well-fed colored people, who were indulging their late-won liberty of travel on the trains, had evidently shirked any responsibilities for such stray remnants of humanity. Slavery was its own provider for old age. There had once been no necessity for the slaves themselves to make provision for winter, as even a squirrel must. They were worse than children now, and far more appealing in their helplessness.

The group slowly departed, and Colonel Bellamy led the way in the opposite direction, toward the ruins of the great house. They crossed the old garden, where some ancient espaliers still clung to the broken brick-work of the walls, and a little fruit still clung to the knotted branches, while great hedges of box, ragged and uncared for, traced the old order of the walks. The heavy dew and warm morning sun brought out that antique fragrance,—the faint pungent odor which wakes the utmost memories of the past. Tom Burton thought with a sudden thrill that the girl with the sweet eyes yesterday had worn a bit of box in her dress. Here and there, under the straying boughs of the shrubbery, bloomed a late scarlet poppy from some scattered seed of which such old soil might well be full. It was a barren, neglected garden enough, but still full of charm and delight, being a garden. There was a fine fragrance of grapes through the undergrowth, but the whole place was completely ruined; a little snake slid from the broken base of a sun-dial; the tall chimneys of the house were already beginning to crumble, and birds and squirrels lived in their crevices and flitted about their lofty tops. At some distance an old negro was singing,—it must have been Milton himself, still unbesought by his dependents, and the song was full of strange, monotonous wails and plaintive cadences, like a lament for war itself, and all the misery that follows in its train.

Colonel Bellamy had not spoken for some moments, but when they reached the terrace which had been before the house there were two flights of stone steps that led to empty air, and these were still adorned by some graceful railings and balusters, bent and rusty and broken.

"You will observe this iron-work, sir," said the Colonel, stopping to regard with pride almost the only relic of the former beauty and state of Fairford. "My grandfather had the pattern carefully planned in Charleston, where such work was formerly well done by Frenchmen." He stopped to point out certain charming features of the design with his walking-stick, and then went on without a glance at the decaying chimneys or the weed-grown cellars and heaps of stones beneath.

The lovely October morning was more than half gone when Milton brought the horse round to the door, and the moment came to say farewell. The Colonel had shown sincere eagerness that the visit should be prolonged for at least another day, but a reason for hurry which the young man hardly confessed to himself was urging him back along the way he had come. He was ready to forget his plans for shooting and wandering eastward on the river shore. He had paid a parting visit to Madam Bellamy in her own room, where she lay on a couch in the sunshine, and had seen the silver cup—a lucky cup he devoutly hoped it might indeed be—on a light stand by her side. It held a few small flowers, as if it had so been brought in to her in the early morning. Her eyes were dim with weeping. She had not thought of its age and history, neither did the sight of such pathetic loot wake bitter feelings against her foes. It was only the cup that her little children had used, one after another, in their babyhood; the last and dearest had kept it longest, and even he was dead—fallen in battle, like the rest.

She wore a hood and wrapping of black lace, which brought out the delicacy of her features like some quaint setting. Her hand trembled as she bade her young guest farewell. As he looked back from the doorway she was like some exiled queen in a peasant's lodging, such dignity and sweet patience were in her look. "I think you bring good fortune," she said. "Nothing can make me so happy as to have my husband find a little pleasure."

As the young man crossed the outer room the familiar eyes of the old portrait caught his own with wistful insistency. He suddenly suspected the double reason: he had been dreaming of other eyes, and knew that his fellow-traveler had kept him company. "Madam Bellamy," he said, turning back, and blushing as he bent to speak to her in a lower voice,—"the portrait; is it like any one? is it like your granddaughter? Could I have seen her on my way here?"

Madam Bellamy looked up at his eager face with a light of unwonted pleasure in her eyes. "Yes," said she, "my granddaughter would have been on her way to Whitfields. She has always been thought extremely like the picture: it is her great-grandmother. Good-by; pray let us see you at Fairford again;" and they said farewell once more, while Tom Burton promised something, half to himself, about the Christmas hunt, he whispered, and a most lovely hope was in his heart.

"You have been most welcome," said the Colonel at parting. "I beg that you will be so kind as to repeat this visit. I shall hope that we may have some shooting together."

"I shall hope so too," answered Tom Burton, warmly. Then, acting from sudden impulse, he quickly unslung his gun, and begged his old friend to keep it—to use it, at any rate, until he came again.

The old Virginian did not reply for a moment. "Your grandfather would have done this, sir. I loved him, and I take it from you both. My own gun is too poor a thing to offer in return." His voice shook; it was the only approach to a lament, to a complaint, that he had made.

This was the moment of farewell; the young man held the Colonel's hand in a boyish eager grasp. "I wish that I might be like a son to you," he said. "May I write, sometimes, and may I really come to Fairford again?"

The old Colonel answered him most affectionately, "Oh yes; we must think of the Christmas hunt," he said, and so they parted.

Tom Burton rode slowly away, and presently the fireless chimneys of Fairford were lost to sight behind the clustering trees. The noonday light was shining on the distant river; the road was untraveled and untenanted for miles together, except by the Northern rider and his Southern steed.

THE HILTONS' HOLIDAY

I

There was a bright, full moon in the clear sky, and the sunset was still shining faintly in the west. Dark woods stood all about the old Hilton farmhouse, save down the hill, westward, where lay the shadowy fields which John Hilton, and his father before him, had cleared and tilled with much toil,—the small fields to which they had given the industry and even affection of their honest lives.

John Hilton was sitting on the doorstep of his house. As he moved his head in and out of the shadows, turning now and then to speak to his wife, who sat just within the doorway, one could see his good face, rough and somewhat unkempt, as if he were indeed a creature of the shady woods and brown earth, instead of the noisy town. It was late in the long spring evening, and he had just come from the lower field as cheerful as a boy, proud of having finished the planting of his potatoes.

"I had to do my last row mostly by feelin'," he said to his wife. "I'm proper glad I pushed through, an' went back an' ended off after supper. 'T would have taken me a good part o' to-morrow mornin', an' broke my day."

"'T ain't no use for ye to work yourself all to pieces, John," answered the woman quickly. "I declare it does seem harder than ever that we couldn't have kep' our boy; he'd been comin' fourteen years old this fall, most a grown man, and he'd work right 'longside of ye now the whole time."

"'T was hard to lose him; I do seem to miss little John," said the father sadly. "I expect there was reasons why 't was best. I feel able an' smart to work; my father was a girt strong man, an' a monstrous worker afore me. 'T ain't that; but I was thinkin' by myself to-day what a sight o' company the boy would ha' been. You know, small's he was, how I could trust to leave him anywhere with the team, and how he'd beseech to go with me wherever I was goin'; always right in my tracks I used to tell 'em. Poor little John, for all he was so young he had a great deal o' judgment; he'd ha' made a likely man."

The mother sighed heavily as she sat within the shadow.

"But then there's the little girls, a sight o' help an' company," urged the father eagerly, as if it were wrong to dwell upon sorrow and loss. "Katy, she's most as good as a boy, except that she ain't very rugged. She's a real little farmer, she's helped me a sight this spring; an' you've got Susan Ellen, that makes a complete little housekeeper for ye as far as she's learnt. I don't see but we're better off than most folks, each on us having a work mate."

"That's so, John," acknowledged Mrs. Hilton wistfully, beginning to rock steadily in her straight, splint-bottomed chair. It was always a good sign when she rocked.

"Where be the little girls so late?" asked their father. "'T is gettin' long past eight o'clock. I don't know when we've all set up so late, but it's so kind o' summer-like an' pleasant. Why, where be they gone?"

"I've told ye; only over to Becker's folks," answered the mother. "I don't see myself what keeps 'em so late; they beseeched me after supper till I let 'em go. They're all in a dazzle with the new teacher; she asked 'em to come over. They say she's unusual smart with 'rethmetic, but she has a kind of a gorpen look to me. She's goin' to give Katy some pieces for her doll, but I told Katy she ought to be ashamed wantin' dolls' pieces, big as she's gettin' to be. I don't know's she ought, though; she ain't but nine this summer."

"Let her take her comfort," said the kind-hearted man. "Them things draws her to the teacher, an' makes them acquainted. Katy's shy with new folks, more so 'n Susan Ellen, who's of the business kind. Katy's shy-feelin' and wishful."

"I don't know but she is," agreed the mother slowly. "Ain't it sing'lar how well acquainted you be with that one, an' I with Susan Ellen? 'T was always so from the first. I'm doubtful sometimes our Katy ain't one that'll be like to get married—anyways not about here. She lives right with herself, but Susan Ellen ain't nothin' when she's alone, she's always after company; all the boys is waitin' on her a'ready. I ain't afraid but she'll take her pick when the time comes. I expect to see Susan Ellen well settled,—she feels grown up now,—but Katy don't care one mite 'bout none o' them things. She wants to be rovin' out o' doors. I do believe she'd stand an' hark to a bird the whole forenoon."

"Perhaps she'll grow up to be a teacher," suggested John Hilton. "She takes to her book more 'n the other one. I should like one on 'em to be a teacher same's my mother was. They're good girls as anybody's got."

"So they be," said the mother, with unusual gentleness, and the creak of her rocking-chair was heard, regular as the ticking of a clock. The night breeze stirred in the great woods, and the sound of a brook that went falling down the hillside grew louder and louder. Now and then one could hear the plaintive chirp of a bird. The moon glittered with whiteness like a winter moon, and shone upon the low-roofed house until its small window-panes gleamed like silver, and one could almost see the colors of a blooming bush of lilac that grew in a sheltered angle by the kitchen door. There was an incessant sound of frogs in the lowlands.

"Be you sound asleep, John?" asked the wife presently.

"I don't know but what I was a'most," said the tired man, starting a little. "I should laugh if I was to fall sound asleep right here on the step; 't is the bright night, I expect, makes my eyes feel heavy, an' 'tis so peaceful. I was up an' dressed a little past four an' out to work. Well, well!" and he laughed sleepily and rubbed his eyes. "Where's the little girls? I'd better step along an' meet 'em."

"I wouldn't just yet; they'll get home all right, but 't is late for 'em certain. I don't want 'em keepin' Mis' Becker's folks up neither. There, le' 's wait a few minutes," urged Mrs. Hilton.

"I've be'n a-thinkin' all day I'd like to give the child'n some kind of a treat," said the father, wide awake now. "I hurried up my work 'cause I had it so in mind. They don't have the opportunities some do, an' I want 'em to know the world, an' not stay right here on the farm like a couple o' bushes."

"They're a sight better off not to be so full o' notions as some is," protested the mother suspiciously.

"Certain," answered the farmer; "but they're good, bright child'n, an' commencin' to take a sight o' notice. I want 'em to have all we can give 'em. I want 'em to see how other folks does things."

"Why, so do I,"—here the rocking-chair stopped ominously,—"but so long's they're contented"—

"Contented ain't all in this world; hopper-toads may have that quality an' spend all their time a-blinkin'. I don't know's bein' contented is all there is to look for in a child. Ambition's somethin' to me."

"Now you've got your mind on to some plot or other." (The rocking-chair began to move again.) "Why can't you talk right out?"

"'T ain't nothin' special," answered the good man, a little ruffled; he was never prepared for his wife's mysterious powers of divination. "Well there, you do find things out the master! I only thought perhaps I'd take 'em to-morrow, an' go off some where if 't was a good day. I've been promisin' for a good while I'd take 'em to Topham Corners; they've never been there since they was very small."

"I believe you want a good time yourself. You ain't never got over bein' a boy." Mrs. Hilton seemed much amused. "There, go if you want to an' take 'em; they've got their summer hats an' new dresses. I don't know o' nothin' that stands in the way. I should sense it better if there was a circus or anythin' to go to. Why don't you wait an' let the girls pick 'em some strawberries or nice ros' berries, and then they could take an' sell 'em to the stores?"

John Hilton reflected deeply. "I should like to get me some good yellow-turnip seed to plant late. I ain't more 'n satisfied with what I've been gettin' o' late years o' Ira Speed. An' I'm goin' to provide me with a good hoe; mine's gettin' wore out an' all shackly. I can't seem to fix it good."

"Them's excuses," observed Mrs. Hilton, with friendly tolerance. "You just cover up the hoe with somethin', if you get it—I would. Ira Speed's so jealous he'll remember it of you this twenty year, your goin' an' buy in' a new hoe o' anybody but him."

"I've always thought 't was a free country," said John Hilton soberly. "I don't want to vex Ira neither; he favors us all he can in trade. 'T is difficult for him to spare a cent, but he's as honest as daylight."

At this moment there was a sudden sound of young voices, and a pair of young figures came out from the shadow of the woods into the moonlighted open space. An old cock crowed loudly from his perch in the shed, as if he were a herald of royalty. The little girls were hand in hand, and a brisk young dog capered about them as they came.

"Wa'n't it dark gittin' home through the woods this time o' night?" asked the mother hastily, and not without reproach.

"I don't love to have you gone so late; mother an' me was timid about ye, and you've kep' Mis' Becker's folks up, I expect," said their father regretfully. "I don't want to have it said that my little girls ain't got good manners."

"The teacher had a party," chirped Susan Ellen, the elder of the two children. "Goin' home from school she asked the Grover boys, an' Mary an' Sarah Speed. An' Mis' Becker was real pleasant to us: she passed round some cake, an' handed us sap sugar on one of her best plates, an' we played games an' sung some pieces too. Mis' Becker thought we did real well. I can pick out most of a tune on the cabinet organ; teacher says she'll give me lessons."

"I want to know, dear!" exclaimed John Hilton.

"Yes, an' we played Copenhagen, an' took sides spellin', an' Katy beat everybody spellin' there was there."

Katy had not spoken; she was not so strong as her sister, and while Susan Ellen stood a step or two away addressing her eager little audience, Katy had seated herself close to her father on the doorstep. He put his arm around her shoulders, and drew her close to his side, where she stayed.

"Ain't you got nothin' to tell, daughter?" he asked, looking down fondly; and Katy gave a pleased little sigh for answer.

"Tell 'em what's goin' to be the last day o' school, and about our trimmin' the schoolhouse," she said; and Susan Ellen gave the programme in most spirited fashion.

"'T will be a great time," said the mother, when she had finished. "I don't see why folks wants to go trapesin' off to strange places when such things is happenin' right about 'em." But the children did not observe her mysterious air. "Come, you must step yourselves right to bed!"

They all went into the dark, warm house; the bright moon shone upon it steadily all night, and the lilac flowers were shaken by no breath of wind until the early dawn.

II

The Hiltons always waked early. So did their neighbors, the crows and song-sparrows and robins, the light-footed foxes and squirrels in the woods. When John Hilton waked, before five o'clock, an hour later than usual because he had sat up so late, he opened the house door and came out into the yard, crossing the short green turf hurriedly as if the day were too far spent for any loitering. The magnitude of the plan for taking a whole day of pleasure confronted him seriously, but the weather was fair, and his wife, whose disapproval could not have been set aside, had accepted and even smiled upon the great project. It was inevitable now, that he and the children should go to Topham Corners. Mrs. Hilton had the pleasure of waking them, and telling the news.

In a few minutes they came frisking out to talk over the great plans. The cattle were already fed, and their father was milking. The only sign of high festivity was the wagon pulled out into the yard, with both seats put in as if it were Sunday; but Mr. Hilton still wore his every-day clothes, and Susan Ellen suffered instantly from disappointment.

"Ain't we goin', father?" she asked complainingly; but he nodded and smiled at her, even though the cow, impatient to get to pasture, kept whisking her rough tail across his face. He held his head down and spoke cheerfully, in spite of this vexation.

"Yes, sister, we're goin' certain', an' goin' to have a great time too." Susan Ellen thought that he seemed like a boy at that delightful moment, and felt new sympathy and pleasure at once. "You go an' help mother about breakfast an' them things; we want to get off quick 's we can. You coax mother now, both on ye, an' see if she won't go with us."

"She said she wouldn't be hired to," responded Susan Ellen. "She says it's goin' to be hot, an' she's laid out to go over an' see how her aunt Tamsen Brooks is this afternoon."

The father gave a little sigh; then he took heart again. The truth was that his wife made light of the contemplated pleasure, and, much as he usually valued her companionship and approval, he was sure that they should have a better time without her.

It was impossible, however, not to feel guilty of disloyalty at the thought. Even though she might be completely unconscious of his best ideals, he only loved her and the ideals the more, and bent his energies

SARAH ORNE JEWETT

to satisfying her indefinite expectations. His wife still kept much of that youthful beauty which Susan Ellen seemed likely to reproduce.

An hour later the best wagon was ready, and the great expedition set forth. The little dog sat apart, and barked as if it fell entirely upon him to voice the general excitement. Both seats were in the wagon, but the empty place testified to Mrs. Hilton's unyielding disposition. She had wondered why one broad seat would not do, but John Hilton meekly suggested that the wagon looked better with both. The little girls sat on the back seat dressed alike in their Sunday hats of straw with blue ribbons, and their little plaid shawls pinned neatly about their small shoulders. They wore gray thread gloves, and sat very straight. Susan Ellen was half a head the taller, but otherwise, from behind, they looked much alike. As for their father, he was in his Sunday best,—a plain black coat, and a winter hat of felt, which was heavy and rusty-looking for that warm early summer day. He had it in mind to buy a new straw hat at Topham, so that this with the turnip seed and the hoe made three important reasons for going.

"Remember an' lay off your shawls when you get there, an' carry them over your arms," said the mother, clucking like an excited hen to her chickens. "They'll do to keep the dust off your new dresses goin' an' comin'. An' when you eat your dinners don't get spots on you, an' don't point at folks as you ride by, an' stare, or they'll know you come from the country. An' John, you call into Cousin Ad'line Marlow's an' see how they all be, an' tell her I expect her over certain to stop awhile before hayin'. It always eases her phthisic to git up here on the high land, an' I've got a new notion about doin' over her best-room carpet sence I see her that'll save rippin' one breadth. An' don't come home all wore out; an', John, don't you go an' buy me no kickshaws to fetch home. I ain't a child, an' you ain't got no money to waste. I expect you'll go, like's not, an' buy you some kind of a foolish boy's hat; do look an' see if it's reasonable good straw, an' won't splinter all off round the edge. An' you mind, John"—

"Yes, yes, hold on!" cried John impatiently; then he cast a last affectionate, reassuring look at her face, flushed with the hurry and responsibility of starting them off in proper shape. "I wish you was goin' too," he said, smiling. "I do so!" Then the old horse started, and they went out at the bars, and began the careful long descent of the hill. The young dog, tethered to the lilac-bush, was frantic with piteous appeals; the little girls piped their eager good-bys again and again, and their father turned many times to look back and wave his hand. As for their mother, she stood alone and watched them out of sight.

There was one place far out on the high-road where she could catch a last glimpse of the wagon, and she waited what seemed a very long time until it appeared and then was lost to sight again behind a low hill. "They're nothin' but a pack o' child'n together," she said aloud; and then felt lonelier than she expected. She even stooped and patted the unresigned little dog as she passed him, going into the house.

The occasion was so much more important than any one had foreseen that both the little girls were speechless. It seemed at first like going to church in new clothes, or to a funeral; they hardly knew how to behave at the beginning of a whole day of pleasure. They made grave bows at such persons of their acquaintance as happened to be straying in the road. Once or twice they stopped before a farmhouse, while their father talked an inconsiderately long time with some one about the crops and the weather, and even dwelt upon town business and the doings of the selectmen, which might be talked of at any time. The explanations that he gave of their excursion seemed quite unnecessary. It was made entirely clear that he had a little business to do at Topham Corners, and thought he had better give the little girls a ride; they had been very steady at school, and he had finished planting, and could take the day as well as not. Soon, however, they all felt as if such an excursion were an every-day affair, and Susan Ellen began to ask eager questions, while Katy silently sat apart enjoying herself as she never had done before. She liked to see the strange houses, and the children who belonged to them; it was delightful to find flowers that she knew growing all along the road, no matter how far she went from home. Each small homestead looked its best and pleasantest, and shared the exquisite beauty that early summer made,—shared the luxury of greenness and floweriness that decked the rural world. There was an early peony or a late lilac in almost every dooryard.

It was seventeen miles to Topham. After a while they seemed very far from home, having left the hills far behind, and descended to a great level country with fewer tracts of woodland, and wider fields where the crops were much more forward. The houses were all painted, and the roads were smoother and wider. It had been so pleasant driving along that Katy dreaded going into the strange town when she first caught sight of it, though Susan Ellen kept asking with bold fretfulness if they were not almost there. They counted the steeples of four churches, and their father presently showed them the Topham Academy, where their

SARAH ORNE JEWETT

grandmother once went to school, and told them that perhaps some day they would go there too. Katy's heart gave a strange leap; it was such a tremendous thing to think of, but instantly the suggestion was transformed for her into one of the certainties of life. She looked with solemn awe at the tall belfry, and the long rows of windows in the front of the academy, there where it stood high and white among the clustering trees. She hoped that they were going to drive by, but something forbade her taking the responsibility of saying so.

Soon the children found themselves among the crowded village houses. Their father turned to look at them with affectionate solicitude.

"Now sit up straight and appear pretty," he whispered to them. "We're among the best people now, an' I want folks to think well of you."

"I guess we're as good as they be," remarked Susan Ellen, looking at some innocent passers-by with dark suspicion, but Katy tried indeed to sit straight, and folded her hands prettily in her lap, and wished with all her heart to be pleasing for her father's sake. Just then an elderly woman saw the wagon and the sedate party it carried, and smiled so kindly that it seemed to Katy as if Topham Corners had welcomed and received them. She smiled back again as if this hospitable person were an old friend, and entirely forgot that the eyes of all Topham had been upon her.

"There, now we're coming to an elegant house that I want you to see; you'll never forget it," said John Hilton. "It's where Judge Masterson lives, the great lawyer; the handsomest house in the county, everybody says."

"Do you know him, father?" asked Susan Ellen.

"I do," answered John Hilton proudly. "Him and my mother went to school together in their young days, and were always called the two best scholars of their time. The judge called to see her once; he stopped to our house to see her when I was a boy. An' then, some years ago—you've heard me tell how I was on the jury, an' when he heard my name spoken he looked at me sharp, and asked if I wa'n't the son of Catharine Winn, an' spoke most beautiful of your grandmother, an' how well he remembered their young days together."

"I like to hear about that," said Katy.

"She had it pretty hard, I'm afraid, up on the old farm. She was keepin' school in our district when father married her—that's the main reason I backed 'em down when they wanted to tear the old schoolhouse all to pieces," confided John Hilton, turning eagerly.

"They all say she lived longer up here on the hill than she could anywhere, but she never had her health. I wa'n't but a boy when she died. Father an' me lived alone afterward till the time your mother come; 't was a good while, too; I wa'n't married so young as some. 'T was lonesome, I tell you; father was plumb discouraged losin' of his wife, an' her long sickness an' all set him back, an' we'd work all day on the land an' never say a word. I s'pose 't is bein' so lonesome early in life that makes me so pleased to have some nice girls growin' up round me now."

There was a tone in her father's voice that drew Katy's heart toward him with new affection. She dimly understood, but Susan Ellen was less interested. They had often heard this story before, but to one child it was always new and to the other old. Susan Ellen was apt to think it tiresome to hear about her grandmother, who, being dead, was hardly worth talking about.

"There's Judge Masterson's place," said their father in an every-day manner, as they turned a corner, and came into full view of the beautiful old white house standing behind its green trees and terraces and lawns. The children had never imagined anything so stately and fine, and even Susan Ellen exclaimed with pleasure. At that moment they saw an old gentleman, who carried himself with great dignity, coming slowly down the wide box-bordered path toward the gate.

"There he is now, there's the judge!" whispered John Hilton excitedly, reining his horse quickly to the green roadside. "He's goin' down-town to his office; we can wait right here an' see him. I can't expect him to remember me; it's been a good many years. Now you are goin' to see the great Judge Masterson!"

There was a quiver of expectation in their hearts. The judge stopped at his gate, hesitating a moment before he lifted the latch, and glanced up the street at the country wagon with its two prim little girls on the back seat, and the eager man who drove. They seemed to be waiting for something; the old horse was nibbling at the fresh roadside grass. The judge was used to being looked at with interest, and responded now with a smile as he came out to the sidewalk, and unexpectedly turned their way. Then he suddenly lifted his hat with grave politeness, and came directly toward them.

"Good-morning, Mr. Hilton," he said. "I am very glad to see you, sir;" and Mr. Hilton, the little girls' own father, took off his hat with equal courtesy, and bent forward to shake hands.

Susan Ellen cowered and wished herself away, but little Katy sat straighter than ever, with joy in her father's pride and pleasure shining in her pale, flower-like little face.

"These are your daughters, I am sure," said the old gentleman kindly, taking Susan Ellen's limp and reluctant hand; but when he looked at Katy, his face brightened. "How she recalls your mother!" he said with great feeling. "I am glad to see this dear child. You must come to see me with your father, my dear," he added, still looking at her. "Bring both the little girls, and let them run about the old garden; the cherries are just getting ripe," said Judge Masterson hospitably. "Perhaps you will have time to stop this afternoon as you go home?"

"I should call it a great pleasure if you would come and see us again some time. You may be driving our way, sir," said John Hilton.

"Not very often in these days," answered the old judge. "I thank you for the kind invitation. I should like to see the fine view again from your hill westward. Can I serve you in any way while you are in town? Good-by, my little friends!"

Then they parted, but not before Katy, the shy Katy, whose hand the judge still held unconsciously while he spoke, had reached forward as he said good-by, and lifted her face to kiss him. She could not have told why, except that she felt drawn to something in the serious, worn face. For the first time in her life the child had felt the charm of manners; perhaps she owned a kinship between that which made him what he was, and the spark of nobleness and purity in her own simple soul. She turned again and again to look back at him as they drove away.

"Now you have seen one of the first gentlemen in the country," said their father.

"It was worth comin' twice as far"—but he did not say any more, nor turn as usual to look in the children's faces.

In the chief business street of Topham a great many country wagons like the Hiltons' were fastened to the posts, and there seemed to our holiday-makers to be a great deal of noise and excitement.

"Now I've got to do my errands, and we can let the horse rest and feed," said John Hilton. "I'll slip his headstall right off, an' put on his halter. I'm goin' to buy him a real good treat o' oats. First we'll go an' buy me my straw hat; I feel as if this one looked a little past to wear in Topham. We'll buy the things we want, an' then we'll walk all along the street, so you can look in the windows an' see the han'some things, same's your mother likes to. What was it mother told you about your shawls?"

"To take 'em off an' carry 'em over our arms," piped Susan Ellen, without comment, but in the interest of alighting and finding themselves afoot upon the pavement the shawls were forgotten. The children stood at the doorway of a shop while their father went inside, and they tried to see what the Topham shapes of bonnets were like, as their mother had advised them; but everything was exciting and confusing, and they could arrive at no decision. When Mr. Hilton came out with a hat in his hand to be seen in a better light, Katy whispered that she wished he would buy a shiny one like Judge Masterson's; but her father only smiled and shook his head, and said that they were plain folks, he and Katy. There were dry-goods for sale in the same shop, and a young clerk who was measuring linen kindly pulled off some pretty labels with gilded edges and gay pictures, and gave them to the little girls, to their exceeding joy. He may have had small sisters at home, this friendly lad, for he took pains to find two pretty blue boxes besides, and was rewarded by their beaming gratitude.

It was a famous day; they even became used to seeing so many people pass. The village was full of its morning activity, and Susan Ellen gained a new respect for her father, and an increased sense of her own consequence, because even in Topham several persons knew him and called him familiarly by name. The meeting with an old man who had once been a neighbor seemed to give Mr. Hilton the greatest pleasure. The old man called to them from a house doorway as they were passing, and they all went in. The children seated themselves wearily on the wooden step, but their father shook his old friend eagerly by the hand, and declared that he was delighted to see him so well and enjoying the fine weather.

"Oh, yes," said the old man, in a feeble, quavering voice, "I'm astonishin' well for my age. I don't complain, John, I don't complain."

They talked long together of people whom they had known in the past, and Katy, being a little tired, was glad to rest, and sat still with her hands folded, looking about the front yard. There were some kinds of flowers that she never had seen before.

"This is the one that looks like my mother," her father said, and touched Katy's shoulder to remind her to stand up and let herself be seen. "Judge Masterson saw the resemblance; we met him at his gate this morning."

"Yes, she certain does look like your mother, John," said the old man, looking pleasantly at Katy, who found that she liked him better than at first. "She does, certain; the best of young folks is, they remind us of the old ones. 'Tis nateral to cling to life, folks say, but for me, I git impatient at times. Most everybody's gone now, an' I want to be goin'. 'Tis somethin' before me, an' I want to have it over with. I want to be there 'long o' the rest o' the folks. I expect to last quite a while though; I may see ye couple o' times more, John."

John Hilton responded cheerfully, and the children were urged to pick some flowers. The old man awed them with his impatience to be gone. There was such a townful of people about him, and he seemed as lonely as if he were the last survivor of a former world. Until that moment they had felt as if everything were just beginning.

"Now I want to buy somethin' pretty for your mother," said Mr. Hilton, as they went soberly away down the street, the children keeping fast hold of his hands. "By now the old horse will have eat his dinner and had a good rest, so pretty soon we can jog along home. I'm goin' to take you round by the academy, and the old North Meeting-house where Dr. Barstow used to preach. Can't you think o' somethin' that your mother'd want?" he asked suddenly, confronted by a man's difficulty of choice.

"She was talkin' about wantin' a new pepper-box, one day; the top o' the old one won't stay on," suggested Susan Ellen, with delightful readiness. "Can't we have some candy, father?"

"Yes, ma'am," said John Hilton, smiling and swinging her hand to and fro as they walked. "I feel as if some would be good myself. What's all this?" They were passing a photographer's doorway with its enticing array of portraits. "I do declare!" he exclaimed excitedly, "I'm goin' to have our pictures taken; 't will please your mother more 'n a little."

This was, perhaps, the greatest triumph of the day, except the delightful meeting with the judge; they sat in a row, with the father in the middle, and there was no doubt as to the excellence of the likeness. The best hats had to be taken off because they cast a shadow, but they were not missed, as their owners had feared. Both Susan Ellen and Katy looked their brightest and best; their eager young faces would forever shine there; the joy of the holiday was mirrored in the little picture. They did not know why their father was so pleased with it; they would not know until age had dowered them with the riches of association and remembrance.

Just at nightfall the Hiltons reached home again, tired out and happy. Katy had climbed over into the front seat beside her father, because that was always her place when they went to church on Sundays. It was a cool evening, there was a fresh sea wind that brought a light mist with it, and the sky was fast growing cloudy. Somehow the children looked different; it seemed to their mother as if they had grown older and taller since they went away in the morning, and as if they belonged to the town now as much as to the country. The greatness of their day's experience had left her far behind; the day had been silent and lonely without them, and she had had their supper ready, and been watching anxiously, ever since five o'clock. As for the children themselves they had little to say at first they had eaten their luncheon early on the way to Topham. Susan Ellen was childishly cross, but Katy was pathetic and wan. They could hardly wait to show the picture, and their mother was as much pleased as everybody had expected.

"There, what did make you wear your shawls?" she exclaimed a moment afterward, reproachfully. "You ain't been an' wore 'em all day long? I wanted folks to see how pretty your new dresses was, if I did make 'em. Well, well! I wish more 'n ever now I'd gone an' seen to ye!"

"An' here's the pepper-box!" said Katy, in a pleased, unconscious tone.

"That really is what I call beautiful," said Mrs. Hilton, after a long and doubtful look. "Our other one was only tin. I never did look so high as a chiny one with flowers, but I can get us another any time for every day. That's a proper hat, as good as you could have got, John. Where's your new hoe?" she asked as he came toward her from the barn, smiling with satisfaction.

"I declare to Moses if I didn't forget all about it," meekly acknowledged the leader of the great excursion. "That an' my yellow turnip seed, too; they went clean out o' my head, there was so many other things to think of. But 't ain't no sort o' matter; I can get a hoe just as well to Ira Speed's."

His wife could not help laughing. "You an' the little girls have had a great time. They was full o' wonder to me about everything, and I expect they'll talk about it for a week. I guess we was right about havin' 'em see somethin' more o' the world."

"Yes," answered John Hilton, with humility, "yes, we did have a beautiful day. I didn't expect so much. They looked as nice as anybody, and appeared so modest an' pretty. The little girls will remember it perhaps by an' by. I guess they won't never forget this day they had 'long o' father."

SARAH ORNE JEWETT

It was evening again, the frogs were piping in the lower meadows, and in the woods, higher up the great hill, a little owl began to hoot. The sea air, salt and heavy, was blowing in over the country at the end of the hot bright day. A lamp was lighted in the house, the happy children were talking together, and supper was waiting. The father and mother lingered for a moment outside and looked down over the shadowy fields; then they went in, without speaking. The great day was over, and they shut the door.

THE ONLY ROSE

I

J ust where the village abruptly ended, and the green mowing fields began, stood Mrs. Bickford's house, looking down the road with all its windows, and topped by two prim chimneys that stood up like ears. It was placed with an end to the road, and fronted southward; you could follow a straight path from the gate past the front door and find Mrs. Bickford sitting by the last window of all in the kitchen, unless she were solemnly stepping about, prolonging the stern duties of her solitary housekeeping.

One day in early summer, when almost every one else in Fairfield had put her house plants out of doors, there were still three flower pots on a kitchen window sill. Mrs. Bickford spent but little time over her rose and geranium and Jerusalem cherry-tree, although they had gained a kind of personality born of long association. They rarely undertook to bloom, but had most courageously maintained life in spite of their owner's unsympathetic but conscientious care. Later in the season she would carry them out of doors, and leave them, until the time of frosts, under the shade of a great apple-tree, where they might make the best of what the summer had to give.

The afternoon sun was pouring in, the Jerusalem cherry-tree drooped its leaves in the heat and looked pale, when a neighbor, Miss Pendexter, came in from the next house but one to make a friendly call. As she passed the parlor with its shut blinds, and the sitting-room, also shaded carefully from the light, she wished, as she had done many times before, that somebody beside the owner might have the pleasure of living in and using so good and pleasant a house. Mrs. Bickford always complained of having so much care, even while she valued herself intelligently upon having the right to do as she pleased with one of the best houses in Fairfield. Miss Pendexter was a cheerful, even gay little person, who always brought a pleasant flurry of excitement, and usually had a genuine though small piece of news to tell, or some new aspect of already received information.

Mrs. Bickford smiled as she looked up to see this sprightly neighbor coming. She had no gift at entertaining herself, and was always glad, as one might say, to be taken off her own hands.

Miss Pendexter smiled back, as if she felt herself to be equal to the occasion.

"How be you to-day?" the guest asked kindly, as she entered the kitchen. "Why, what a sight o' flowers, Mis' Bickford! What be you goin' to do with 'em all?"

Mrs. Bickford wore a grave expression as she glanced over her spectacles. "My sister's boy fetched 'em over," she answered. "You know my sister Parsons's a great hand to raise flowers, an' this boy takes after her. He said his mother thought the gardin never looked handsomer, and she picked me these to send over. They was sendin' a team to Westbury for some fertilizer to put on the land, an' he come with the men, an' stopped to eat his dinner 'long o' me. He's been growin' fast, and looks peaked. I expect sister 'Liza thought the ride, this pleasant day, would do him good. 'Liza sent word for me to come over and pass some days next week, but it ain't so that I can."

"Why, it's a pretty time of year to go off and make a little visit," suggested the neighbor encouragingly.

"I ain't got my sitting-room chamber carpet taken up yet," sighed Mrs. Bickford. "I do feel condemned. I might have done it to-day, but 't was all at end when I saw Tommy coming. There, he's a likely boy, an' so relished his dinner; I happened to be well prepared. I don't know but he's my favorite o' that family. Only I've been sittin' here thinkin', since he went, an' I can't remember that I ever was so belated with my spring cleaning."

"'T was owin' to the weather," explained Miss Pendexter. "None of us could be so smart as common this year, not even the lazy ones that always get one room done the first o' March, and brag of it to others' shame, and then never let on when they do the rest."

The two women laughed together cheerfully. Mrs. Bickford had put up the wide leaf of her large table between the windows and spread out the flowers. She was sorting them slowly into three heaps.

"Why, I do declare if you haven't got a rose in bloom yourself!" exclaimed Miss Pendexter abruptly, as if the bud had not been announced weeks before, and its progress regularly commented upon. "Ain't it a lovely rose? Why, Mis' Bickford!"

"Yes 'm, it's out to-day," said Mrs. Bickford, with a somewhat plaintive air. "I'm glad you come in so as to see it."

The bright flower was like a face. Somehow, the beauty and life of it were surprising in the plain room, like a gay little child who might suddenly appear in a doorway. Miss Pendexter forgot herself and her hostess and the tangled mass of garden flowers in looking at the red

SARAH ORNE JEWETT

rose. She even forgot that it was incumbent upon her to carry forward the conversation. Mrs. Bickford was subject to fits of untimely silence which made her friends anxiously sweep the corners of their minds in search of something to say, but any one who looked at her now could easily see that it was not poverty of thought that made her speechless, but an overburdening sense of the inexpressible.

"Goin' to make up all your flowers into bo'quets? I think the short-stemmed kinds is often pretty in a dish," suggested Miss Pendexter compassionately.

"I thought I should make them into three bo'quets. I wish there wa'n't quite so many. Sister Eliza's very lavish with her flowers; she's always been a kind sister, too," said Mrs. Bickford vaguely. She was not apt to speak with so much sentiment, and as her neighbor looked at her narrowly she detected unusual signs of emotion. It suddenly became evident that the three nosegays were connected in her mind with her bereavement of three husbands, and Miss Pendexter's easily roused curiosity was quieted by the discovery that her friend was bent upon a visit to the burying-ground. It was the time of year when she was pretty sure to spend an afternoon there, and sometimes they had taken the walk in company. Miss Pendexter expected to receive the usual invitation, but there was nothing further said at the moment, and she looked again at the pretty rose.

Mrs. Bickford aimlessly handled the syringas and flowering almond sprays, choosing them out of the fragrant heap only to lay them down again. She glanced out of the window; then gave Miss Pendexter a long expressive look.

"I expect you're going to carry 'em over to the burying-ground?" inquired the guest, in a sympathetic tone.

"Yes 'm," said the hostess, now well started in conversation and in quite her every-day manner. "You see I was goin' over to my brother's folks to-morrow in South Fairfield, to pass the day; they said they were goin' to send over to-morrow to leave a wagon at the blacksmith's, and they'd hitch that to their best chaise, so I could ride back very comfortable. You know I have to avoid bein' out in the mornin' sun?"

Miss Pendexter smiled to herself at this moment; she was obliged to move from her chair at the window, the May sun was so hot on her back, for Mrs. Bickford always kept the curtains rolled high up, out of the way, for fear of fading and dust. The kitchen was a blaze of light. As for the Sunday chaise being sent, it was well known that Mrs. Bickford's married brothers and sisters comprehended the truth that she was a woman of property, and had neither chick nor child.

"So I thought 't was a good opportunity to just stop an' see if the lot was in good order,—last spring Mr. Wallis's stone hove with the frost; an' so I could take these flowers." She gave a sigh. "I ain't one that can bear flowers in a close room,—they bring on a headache; but I enjoy 'em as much as anybody to look at, only you never know what to put 'em in. If I could be out in the mornin' sun, as some do, and keep flowers in the house, I should have me a gardin, certain," and she sighed again.

"A garden's a sight o' care, but I don't begrudge none o' the care I give to mine. I have to scant on flowers so 's to make room for pole beans," said Miss Pendexter gayly. She had only a tiny strip of land behind her house, but she always had something to give away, and made riches out of her narrow poverty. "A few flowers gives me just as much pleasure as more would," she added. "You get acquainted with things when you've only got one or two roots. My sweet-williams is just like folks."

"Mr. Bickford was partial to sweet-williams," said Mrs. Bickford. "I never knew him to take notice of no other sort of flowers. When we'd be over to Eliza's, he'd walk down her gardin, an' he'd never make no comments until he come to them, and then he'd say, 'Those is sweet-williams.' How many times I've heard him!"

"You ought to have a sprig of 'em for his bo'quet," suggested Miss Pendexter.

"Yes, I've put a sprig in," said her companion.

At this moment Miss Pendexter took a good look at the bouquets, and found that they were as nearly alike as careful hands could make them. Mrs. Bickford was evidently trying to reach absolute impartiality.

"I don't know but you think it's foolish to tie 'em up this afternoon," she said presently, as she wound the first with a stout string. "I thought I could put 'em in a bucket o' water out in the shed, where there's a draught o' air, and then I should have all my time in the morning. I shall have a good deal to do before I go. I always sweep the setting-room and front entry Wednesdays. I want to leave everything nice, goin' away for all day so. So I meant to get the flowers out o' the way this afternoon. Why, it's most half past four, ain't it? But I sha'n't pick the rose till mornin'; 't will be blowed out better then."

"The rose?" questioned Miss Pendexter. "Why, are you goin' to pick that, too?"

"Yes, I be. I never like to let 'em fade on the bush. There, that's just what's a-troublin' me," and she turned to give a long, imploring look at the friend who sat beside her. Miss Pendexter had moved her chair before the table in order to be out of the way of the sun. "I don't seem to know which of 'em ought to have it," said Mrs. Bickford despondently. "I do so hate to make a choice between 'em; they all had their good points, especially Mr. Bickford, and I respected 'em all. I don't know but what I think of one on 'em 'most as much as I do of the other."

"Why, 'tis difficult for you, ain't it?" responded Miss Pendexter. "I don't know's I can offer advice."

"No, I s'pose not," answered her friend slowly, with a shadow of disappointment coming over her calm face. "I feel sure you would if you could, Abby."

Both of the women felt as if they were powerless before a great emergency.

"There's one thing,—they're all in a better world now," said Miss Pendexter, in a self-conscious and constrained voice; "they can't feel such little things or take note o' slights same's we can."

"No; I suppose 't is myself that wants to be just," answered Mrs. Bickford. "I feel under obligations to my last husband when I look about and see how comfortable he left me. Poor Mr. Wallis had his great projects, an' perhaps if he'd lived longer he'd have made a record; but when he died he'd failed all up, owing to that patent corn-sheller he'd put everything into, and, as you know, I had to get along 'most any way I could for the next few years. Life was very disappointing with Mr. Wallis, but he meant well, an' used to be an amiable person to dwell with, until his temper got spoilt makin' so many hopes an' havin' 'em turn out failures. He had consider'ble of an air, an' dressed very handsome when I was first acquainted with him, Mr. Wallis did. I don't know's you ever knew Mr. Wallis in his prime?"

"He died the year I moved over here from North Denfield," said Miss Pendexter, in a tone of sympathy. "I just knew him by sight. I was to his funeral. You know you lived in what we call the Wells house then, and I felt it wouldn't be an intrusion, we was such near neighbors. The first time I ever was in your house was just before that, when he was sick, an' Mary 'Becca Wade an' I called to see if there was anything we could do."

"They used to say about town that Mr. Wallis went to an' fro like a mail-coach an' brought nothin' to pass," announced Mrs. Bickford without bitterness. "He ought to have had a better chance than he did in this little neighborhood. You see, he had excellent ideas, but he never'd learned the machinist's trade, and there was somethin' the matter with every model he contrived. I used to be real narrow-minded when he talked about moving 'way up to Lowell, or some o' them places; I hated to think of leaving my folks; and now I see that I never done right by him. His ideas was good. I know once he was on a jury, and there was a man stopping to the tavern where he was, near the court house, a man that traveled for a firm to Lowell; and they engaged in talk, an' Mr. Wallis let out some o' his notions an' contrivances, an' he said that man wouldn't hardly stop to eat, he was so interested, an' said he'd look for a chance for him up to Lowell. It all sounded so well that I kind of begun to think about goin' myself. Mr. Wallis said we'd close the house here, and go an' board through the winter. But he never heard a word from him, and the disappointment was one he never got over. I think of it now different from what I did then. I often used to be kind of disapproving to Mr. Wallis; but there, he used to be always tellin' over his great projects. Somebody told me once that a man by the same name of the one he met while he was to court had got some patents for the very things Mr. Wallis used to be workin' over; but 't was after he died, an' I don't know's 't was in him to ever really set things up so other folks could ha' seen their value. His machines always used to work kind of rickety, but folks used to come from all round to see 'em; they was curiosities if they wa'n't nothin' else, an' gave him a name."

Mrs. Bickford paused a moment, with some geranium leaves in her hand, and seemed to suppress with difficulty a desire to speak even more freely.

"He was a dreadful notional man," she said at last, regretfully, and as if this fact were a poor substitute for what had just been in her mind. "I recollect one time he worked all through the early winter over my churn, an' got it so it would go three quarters of an hour all of itself if you wound it up; an' if you'll believe it, he went an' spent all that time for nothin' when the cow was dry, an' we was with difficulty borrowin' a pint o' milk a day somewheres in the neighborhood just to get along with." Mrs. Bickford flushed with displeasure, and turned to look at her visitor. "Now what do you think of such a man as that, Miss Pendexter?" she asked.

"Why, I don't know but 't was just as good for an invention," answered Miss Pendexter timidly; but her friend looked doubtful, and did not appear to understand.

SARAH ORNE JEWETT

"Then I asked him where it was, one day that spring when I'd got tired to death churnin', an' the butter wouldn't come in a churn I'd had to borrow, and he'd gone an' took ours all to pieces to get the works to make some other useless contrivance with. He had no sort of a business turn, but he was well meanin', Mr. Wallis was, an' full o' divertin' talk; they used to call him very good company. I see now that he never had no proper chance. I've always regretted Mr. Wallis," said she who was now the widow Bickford.

"I'm sure you always speak well of him," said Miss Pendexter. "'T was a pity he hadn't got among good business men, who could push his inventions an' do all the business part."

"I was left very poor an' needy for them next few years," said Mrs. Bickford mournfully; "but he never'd give up but what he should die worth his fifty thousand dollars. I don't see now how I ever did get along them next few years without him; but there, I always managed to keep a pig, an' sister Eliza gave me my potatoes, and I made out somehow. I could dig me a few greens, you know, in spring, and then 't would come strawberry-time, and other berries a-followin' on. I was always decent to go to meetin' till within the last six months, an' then I went in bad weather, when folks wouldn't notice; but 't was a rainy summer, an' I managed to get considerable preachin' after all. My clothes looked proper enough when 't was a wet Sabbath. I often think o' them pinched days now, when I'm left so comfortable by Mr. Bickford."

"Yes 'm, you've everything to be thankful for," said Miss Pendexter, who was as poor herself at that moment as her friend had ever been, and who could never dream of venturing upon the support and companionship of a pig. "Mr. Bickford was a very personable man," she hastened to say, the confidences were so intimate and interesting.

"Oh, very," replied Mrs. Bickford; "there was something about him that was very marked. Strangers would always ask who he was as he come into meetin'. His words counted; he never spoke except he had to. 'T was a relief at first after Mr. Wallis's being so fluent; but Mr. Wallis was splendid company for winter evenings,—'t would be eight o'clock before you knew it. I didn't use to listen to it all, but he had a great deal of information. Mr. Bickford was dreadful dignified; I used to be sort of meechin' with him along at the first, for fear he'd disapprove of me; but I found out 'twa'n't no need; he was always just that way, an' done everything by rule an' measure. He hadn't the mind of my other husbands, but he was a very dignified appearing man; he used 'most always to sleep in the evenin's, Mr. Bickford did."

"Them is lovely bo'quets, certain!" exclaimed Miss Pendexter. "Why, I couldn't tell 'em apart; the flowers are comin' out just right, aren't they?"

Mrs. Bickford nodded assent, and then, startled by sudden recollection, she cast a quick glance at the rose in the window.

"I always seem to forget about your first husband, Mr. Fraley," Miss Pendexter suggested bravely. "I've often heard you speak of him, too, but he'd passed away long before I ever knew you."

"He was but a boy," said Mrs. Bickford. "I thought the world was done for me when he died, but I've often thought since 't was a mercy for him. He come of a very melancholy family, and all his brothers an' sisters enjoyed poor health; it might have been his lot. Folks said we was as pretty a couple as ever come into church; we was both dark, with black eyes an' a good deal o' color,—you wouldn't expect it to see me now. Albert was one that held up his head, and looked as if he meant to own the town, an' he had a good word for everybody. I don't know what the years might have brought."

There was a long pause. Mrs. Bickford leaned over to pick up a heavy-headed Guelder-rose that had dropped on the floor.

"I expect 't was what they call fallin' in love," she added, in a different tone; "he wa'n't nothin' but a boy, an' I wa'n't nothin' but a girl, but we was dreadful happy. He didn't favor his folks,—they all had hay-colored hair and was faded-looking, except his mother; they was alike, and looked alike, an' set everything by each other. He was just the kind of strong, hearty young man that goes right off if they get a fever. We was just settled on a little farm, an' he'd have done well if he'd had time; as it was, he left debts. He had a hasty temper, that was his great fault, but Albert had a lovely voice to sing; they said there wa'n't no such tenor voice this part o' the State. I could hear him singin' to himself right out in the field a-ploughin' or hoein', an' he didn't know it half o' the time, no more 'n a common bird would. I don't know's I valued his gift as I ought to, but there was nothin' ever sounded so sweet to me. I ain't one that ever had much fancy, but I knowed Albert had a pretty voice."

Mrs. Bickford's own voice trembled a little, but she held up the last bouquet and examined it critically. "I must hurry now an' put these in water," she said, in a matter of fact tone. Little Miss Pendexter was so quiet and sympathetic that her hostess felt no more embarrassed than if she had been talking only to herself.

SARAH ORNE JEWETT

"Yes, they do seem to droop some; 't is a little warm for them here in the sun," said Miss Pendexter; "but you'll find they'll all come up if you give them their fill o' water. They'll look very handsome to-morrow; folks'll notice them from the road. You've arranged them very tasty, Mis' Bickford."

"They do look pretty, don't they?" Mrs. Bickford regarded the three in turn. "I want to have them all pretty. You may deem it strange, Abby."

"Why, no, Mis' Bickford," said the guest sincerely, although a little perplexed by the solemnity of the occasion. "I know how 'tis with friends,—that having one don't keep you from wantin' another; 'tis just like havin' somethin' to eat, and then wantin' somethin' to drink just the same. I expect all friends find their places."

But Mrs. Bickford was not interested in this figure, and still looked vague and anxious as she began to brush the broken stems and wilted leaves into her wide calico apron. "I done the best I could while they was alive," she said, "and mourned 'em when I lost 'em, an' I feel grateful to be left so comfortable now when all is over. It seems foolish, but I'm still at a loss about that rose."

"Perhaps you'll feel sure when you first wake up in the morning," answered Miss Pendexter solicitously. "It's a case where I don't deem myself qualified to offer you any advice. But I'll say one thing, seeing's you've been so friendly spoken and confiding with me. I never was married myself, Mis' Bickford, because it wa'n't so that I could have the one I liked."

"I suppose he ain't livin', then? Why, I wa'n't never aware you had met with a disappointment, Abby," said Mrs. Bickford instantly. None of her neighbors had ever suspected little Miss Pendexter of a romance.

"Yes 'm, he's livin'," replied Miss Pendexter humbly. "No 'm, I never have heard that he died."

"I want to know!" exclaimed the woman of experience. "Well, I'll tell you this, Abby: you may have regretted your lot, and felt lonesome and hardshipped, but they all have their faults, and a single woman's got her liberty, if she ain't got other blessin's."

"'T wouldn't have been my choice to live alone," said Abby, meeker than before. "I feel very thankful for my blessin's, all the same. You've always been a kind neighbor, Mis' Bickford."

"Why can't you stop to tea?" asked the elder woman, with unusual cordiality; but Miss Pendexter remembered that her hostess often expressed a dislike for unexpected company, and promptly took her departure after she had risen to go, glancing up at the bright flower as she passed outside the window. It seemed to belong most to Albert, but she had not liked to say so. The sun was low; the green fields stretched away southward into the misty distance.

II

M rs. Bickford's house appeared to watch her out of sight down the road, the next morning. She had lost all spirit for her holiday. Perhaps it was the unusual excitement of the afternoon's reminiscences, or it might have been simply the bright moonlight night which had kept her broad awake until dawn, thinking of the past, and more and more concerned about the rose. By this time it had ceased to be merely a flower, and had become a definite symbol and assertion of personal choice. She found it very difficult to decide. So much of her present comfort and well-being was due to Mr. Bickford; still, it was Mr. Wallis who had been most unfortunate, and to whom she had done least justice. If she owed recognition to Mr. Bickford, she certainly owed amends to Mr. Wallis. If she gave him the rose, it would be for the sake of affectionate apology. And then there was Albert, to whom she had no thought of being either indebted or forgiving. But she could not escape from the terrible feeling of indecision.

It was a beautiful morning for a drive, but Mrs. Bickford was kept waiting some time for the chaise. Her nephew, who was to be her escort, had found much social advantage at the blacksmith's shop, so that it was after ten when she finally started with the three large flat-backed bouquets, covered with a newspaper to protect them from the sun. The petals of the almond flowers were beginning to scatter, and now and then little streams of water leaked out of the newspaper and trickled down the steep slope of her best dress to the bottom of the chaise. Even yet she had not made up her mind; she had stopped trying to deal with such an evasive thing as decision, and leaned back and rested as best she could.

"What an old fool I be!" she rebuked herself from time to time, in so loud a whisper that her companion ventured a respectful "What, ma'am?" and was astonished that she made no reply. John was a handsome young man, but Mrs. Bickford could never cease thinking of him as a boy. He had always been her favorite among the younger members of the family, and now returned this affectionate feeling, being possessed of an instinctive confidence in the sincerities of his prosaic aunt.

As they drove along, there had seemed at first to be something unsympathetic and garish about the beauty of the summer day. After the shade and shelter of the house, Mrs. Bickford suffered even more from a contracted and assailed feeling out of doors. The very trees by the roadside had a curiously fateful, trying way of standing back to watch her, as she passed in the acute agony of indecision, and she was annoyed and startled by a bird that flew too near the chaise in a moment of surprise. She was conscious of a strange reluctance to the movement of the Sunday chaise, as if she were being conveyed against her will; but the companionship of her nephew John grew every moment to be more and more a reliance. It was very comfortable to sit by his side, even though he had nothing to say; he was manly and cheerful, and she began to feel protected.

"Aunt Bickford," he suddenly announced, "I may's well out with it! I've got a piece o' news to tell you, if you won't let on to nobody. I expect you'll laugh, but you know I've set everything by Mary Lizzie Gifford ever since I was a boy. Well, sir!"

"Well, sir!" exclaimed aunt Bickford in her turn, quickly roused into most comfortable self-forgetfulness. "I am really pleased. She'll make you a good, smart wife, John. Ain't all the folks pleased, both sides?"

"Yes, they be," answered John soberly, with a happy, important look that became him well.

"I guess I can make out to do something for you to help along, when the right time comes," said aunt Bickford impulsively, after a moment's reflection. "I've known what it is to be starting out in life with plenty o' hope. You ain't calculatin' on gettin' married before fall,—or be ye?"

"'Long in the fall," said John regretfully. "I wish t' we could set up for ourselves right away this summer. I ain't got much ahead, but I can work well as anybody, an' now I'm out o' my time."

"She's a nice, modest, pretty girl. I thought she liked you, John," said the old aunt. "I saw her over to your mother's, last day I was there. Well, I expect you'll be happy."

"Certain," said John, turning to look at her affectionately, surprised by this outspokenness and lack of embarrassment between them. "Thank you, aunt," he said simply; "you're a real good friend to me;" and he looked away again hastily, and blushed a fine scarlet over his sun-browned face. "She's coming over to spend the day with the girls," he added. "Mother thought of it. You don't get over to see us very often."

Mrs. Bickford smiled approvingly. John's mother looked for her good opinion, no doubt, but it was very proper for John to have told his prospects himself, and in such a pretty way. There was no shilly-shallying about the boy.

"My gracious!" said John suddenly. "I'd like to have drove right by the burying-ground. I forgot we wanted to stop."

Strange as it may appear, Mrs. Bickford herself had not noticed the burying-ground, either, in her excitement and pleasure; now she felt distressed and responsible again, and showed it in her face at once. The young man leaped lightly to the ground, and reached for the flowers.

"Here, you just let me run up with 'em," he said kindly. "'T is hot in the sun to-day, an' you'll mind it risin' the hill. We'll stop as I fetch you back to-night, and you can go up comfortable an' walk the yard after sundown when it's cool, an' stay as long as you're a mind to. You seem sort of tired, aunt."

"I don't know but what I will let you carry 'em," said Mrs. Bickford slowly.

To leave the matter of the rose in the hands of fate seemed weakness and cowardice, but there was not a moment for consideration. John was a smiling fate, and his proposition was a great relief. She watched him go away with a terrible inward shaking, and sinking of pride. She had held the flowers with so firm a grasp that her hands felt weak and numb, and as she leaned back and shut her eyes she was afraid to open them again at first for fear of knowing the bouquets apart even at that distance, and giving instructions which she might regret. With a sudden impulse she called John once or twice eagerly; but her voice had a thin and piping sound, and the meditative early crickets that chirped in the fresh summer grass probably sounded louder in John's ears. The bright light on the white stones dazzled Mrs. Bickford's eyes; and then all at once she felt light-hearted, and the sky seemed to lift itself higher and wider from the earth, and she gave a sigh of relief as her messenger came back along the path. "I know who I do hope's got the right one," she said to herself. "There, what a touse I be in! I don't see what I had to go and pick the old rose for, anyway."

"I declare, they did look real handsome, aunt," said John's hearty voice as he approached the chaise. "I set 'em up just as you told me. This one fell out, an' I kept it. I don't know's you'll care. I can give it to Lizzie."

He faced her now with a bright, boyish look. There was something gay in his buttonhole,—it was the red rose.

Aunt Bickford blushed like a girl. "Your choice is easy made," she faltered mysteriously, and then burst out laughing, there in front of the burying-ground. "Come, get right in, dear," she said. "Well, well! I guess the rose was made for you; it looks very pretty in your coat, John."

She thought of Albert, and the next moment the tears came into her old eyes. John was a lover, too.

"My first husband was just such a tall, straight young man as you be," she said as they drove along. "The flower he first give me was a rose."

A SECOND SPRING

I

The Haydon farm was only a few miles from the sea, and the spring wind, which had been blowing from the south all day, had gone into the east. A chilly salt fog had begun to come in, creeping along where a brook wound among the lower fields, like a ghostly serpent that was making its way to shelter across the country.

The old Haydon house stood on high rising land, with two great walnut-trees at one side, and a tall, thin, black-looking spruce in front that had lost its mate. A comfortable row of round-headed old apple-trees led all the way up a long lane from the main road. This lane and the spacious side yard were scarred by wheel ruts, and the fresh turf was cut up by the stamping feet of many horses. It was the evening of a sad day,—the evening after Israel Haydon's wife's funeral. Many of the people who were present had far to go, and so the funeral feast had been served early.

THE OLD PLACE LOOKED DESERTED. The dandelions, which had shone so bright in the grass that morning, were all shut up, and the syringa bushes in the front yard seemed to have taken back their rash buds, and to have grown as gray as winter again. The light was failing fast out of doors; there was a lamp lighted in the kitchen, and a figure kept passing between it and the window.

Israel Haydon lingered as long as he could over his barn-work. Somehow it seemed lonely in the barn, and as long as he could see or feel his way about, he kept himself busy over the old horse and cow, accepting their inexpressive companionship, and serving their suppers with unusual generosity. His sensations, even of grief, were not very distinct to him; there was only a vague sense of discomfort, of being disturbed in his quiet course. He had said to many of his friends that afternoon, "I do' know why 't is, but I can't realize nothing about it," and spoken sincerely; but his face was marked with deep lines; he was suffering deeply from the great loss that had befallen him.

His wife had been a woman of uncommon social gifts and facilities, and he had missed her leadership in the great occasion that was just over. Everybody had come to him for directions, and expected from him the knowledge of practical arrangements that she had always shown in the forty years of their married life. He had forgotten already that it was a worn-out and suffering woman who had died; the remembrance of long weeks of illness faded from his mind. It appeared to him as if, in her most active and busy aspect, she had suddenly vanished out of the emergencies and close dependence of their every-day lives.

Mr. Haydon crossed the yard slowly, after he had locked the barn door and tried the fastening, and then gone back to try it again. He was glad to see the cheerfulness of the lighted kitchen, and to remember that his own sister and the sister of his wife were there in charge and ready to companion him. He could not help a feeling of distress at the thought of entering his lonely home; suddenly the fact of their being there made everything seem worse. Another man might have loitered on the step until he was chilly and miserable, but poor Mr. Haydon only dropped his hand for a moment by his side, and looked away down the lane; then, with bent head, he lifted the latch as he always did, and went in. It seemed as if he consciously shouldered the burden of his loneliness in that dreary moment, and never could stand upright again.

The season of his solitary life began with more cheer than could have been expected. The two women were waiting for him placidly, and did not seem to be curious how he might be bearing this great disaster. They had cleared away all signs of the great company, and the kitchen looked as it always did; it had not occurred to them to occupy the more formal sitting-room. The warmth of the fire was pleasant; a table was spread with supper. One of the women was bringing the teapot from the stove, and the other was placidly knitting a blue yarn stocking. It seemed as if Martha Haydon herself might at any moment come out of the pantry door or up the cellar stairs.

"We was just about ready for you, Isr'el," said his sister-in-law Stevens, glancing at him eagerly. "We didn't stop to take anything ourselves this afternoon, and we didn't suppose 't was so you could; an' we thought we'd just make a quiet cup o' tea when we had everything put to rights, and could set down an' enjoy it. Now you draw right up to the table; that's clever; 't will do us all good."

The good woman bore some likeness to her sister just departed; Israel had never noticed it so much before. She had a comfortable, motherly way, and his old face twitched in spite of himself as he bent over the brimming and smoking cup that she handed across the square table.

"I declare!" said his own sister, Mrs. Abby Martin. "We could reckon what a sight o' folks there was here this afternoon by the times we had to make new tea, if there wa'n't no other way. I don't know's I ever see a larger gathering on such an occasion. Mis' Stevens an' me was trying to count 'em. There was twenty-six wagons hitched in the yard an' lane, so William said, besides all that come afoot; an' a few had driven away before they made the count."

"I'd no idea of there bein' so many," said Israel sadly. "Well, 't was natural for all who knew her to show respect. I felt much obliged to the folks, and for Elder Wall's excellent remarks."

"A number spoke their approval to him in my hearing. He seemed pleased that everything passed off well," said sister Martin. "I expect he wanted to do the best he could. Everybody knows she was always a good friend to him. I never see anybody that set so by her minister. William was telling of me he'd been very attentive all through her sickness. Poor William! He does mourn, but he behaved very pretty, I thought. He wanted us to tell you that he'd be over to-morrow soon's he could. He wanted dreadful to stop with ye overnight, but we all know what it is to run a milk farm."

"I'd b'en glad if 't was so he could be here with us to-night, an' his wife with him," said the old man, pushing away his cup. The remnants of the afternoon feast, with which the table was spread, failed to tempt his appetite. He rose and took his old wooden armchair by the stove, and clasped his hands before him. The long brown fingers began to play mechanically upon each other. It was strange how these trivial, unconscious habits continued in spite of the great change which had shaken his life to its foundations.

II

At noon the next day Israel Haydon and his son William came up across the field together. They had on their every-day clothes, and were talking about every-day matters as they walked along. Mr. Haydon himself had always looked somewhat unlike a farmer, even though there had been no more diligent and successful tiller of the soil in the town of Atfield. He never had bought himself a rougher suit of clothes or a coarse hat for haying, but his discarded Sunday best in various states of decadence served him for barn and field. It was proverbial that a silk hat lasted him five years for best and ten for common; but whatever he might be doing, Israel Haydon always preserved an air of unmistakable dignity. He was even a little ministerial in his look; there had been a minister in the family two or three generations back. Mr. Haydon and his wife had each inherited some money. They were by nature thrifty, and now their only son was well married, with a good farm of his own, to which Israel had added many acres of hay land and tillage, saying that he was getting old, and was going to take the rest of his life easily. In this way the old people had thrown many of their worldly cares upon their son's broad shoulders. They had paid visits each summer to their kindred in surrounding towns, starting off in their Sunday chaise with sober pleasure, serene in their prosperity, and free from any dark anticipations, although they could not bring themselves to consent to any long absence, and the temptation of going to see friends in the West was never dangerous to their peace of mind. But the best of their lives was apparently still before them, when good Martha Haydon's strength mysteriously failed; and one dark day the doctor, whom Israel Haydon had anxiously questioned behind the wood-pile, just out of sight from his wife's window—the doctor had said that she never would be any better. The downfall of his happiness had been swift and piteous. William Haydon was a much larger and rosier man than his father had ever been; the old man looked shrunken as they crossed the field together. They had prolonged their talk about letting the great south field lie fallow, and about some new Hereford cattle that the young farmer had just bought, until nothing more was left to say on either side. Then there came a long pause, when each waited for the other to speak. William grew impatient at last.

"Have you got any notion what it's best to do, sir?" he began boldly; then, finding that his father did not answer, he turned to look at him, and found that the drawn face was set in silent despair.

"I've always been forehanded; I never was caught so unprepared before," he faltered. "'T has been my way, as you know, to think out things beforehand, but it come to the very last before I could give it up 'bout your mother's gettin' better; an' when I did give up, 't wa'n't so I could think o' anything. An' here's your aunts got their families dependin' on 'em, and wantin' to git away soon as may be. I don't know which way to look."

"Marilla and I should be thankful if you'd come and stop 'long of us this winter"—the younger man began, eagerly.

"No, no!" said his father sternly. "I ain't goin' to live in the chimbly-corner of another man's house. I ain't but a little past sixty-seven. I've got to stand in my lot an' place. 'T wouldn't be neither your house nor mine, William," he said, in a softer tone. "You're a good son; your mother always said you was a good son."

Israel Haydon's voice broke, and William Haydon's eyes filled with tears, and they plodded along together in the soft spring grass.

"I've gone over everything I wish I could forget—all the bothering tricks I played her, 'way back when I was a boy," said the young man, with great feeling. "I declare, I don't know what to do, I miss her so."

"You was an only child," said the father solemnly; "we done the best we could by ye. She often said you was a good son, and she wa'n't surprised to see ye prosper. An' about Marilly, 'long at the first, when you was courtin' her, 't was only that poor mother thought nobody wa'n't quite good enough for her boy. She come to set everything by Marilly."

The only dark chapter in the family history was referred to for the last time, to be forgotten by father and son. The old people had, after all, gloried in their son's bravery in keeping to his own way and choice. The two farms joined. Marilla and her mother were their next neighbors; the mother had since died.

"Father," exclaimed William Haydon suddenly, as they neared the barn, "I do' know now but I've thought o' the very one!"

"What d'ye mean?" said the old man, startled a little by such vehemence.

"'T ain't nobody I feel sure of getting," explained the son, his ardor suddenly cooling. "I had Maria Durrant in my mind—Marilla's cousin. Don't you know, she come and stopped with us six weeks that time

Marilla was so dyin' sick and we hadn't been able to get proper help; and what a providence Maria Durrant was! Mother said one day that she never saw so capable a woman."

"I don't stand in need of nursin'," said the old man, grumbling, and taking a defensive attitude of mind. "What's the use, anyway, if you can't get her? I'll contrive to get along somehow. I always have."

William flushed quickly, but made no answer, out of regard to the old man's bereaved and wounded state. He always felt like a schoolboy in his father's presence, though he had for many years been a leader in neighborhood matters, and was at that moment a selectman of the town of Atfield. If he had answered back and entered upon a lively argument it probably would have done the old man good; anything would have seemed better than the dull hunger in his heart, the impossibility of forming new habits of life, which made a wall about his very thoughts.

After a surly silence, when the son was needlessly repentant and the father's face grew cloudy with disapproval, the two men parted. William had made arrangements to stay all the afternoon, but he now found an excuse for going to the village, and drove away down the lane. He had not turned into the highroad before he wished himself back again, while Israel Haydon looked after him reproachfully, more lonely than ever, in the sense that something had come between them, though he could not tell exactly what. The spring fields lay broad and green in the sunshine; there was a cheerful sound of frogs in the lower meadow.

"Poor mother! how she did love early weather like this!" he said, half aloud. "She'd been getting out to the door twenty times a day, just to have a look. An' how she'd laugh to hear the frogs again! Oh, poor me! poor me!" For the first time he found himself in tears. The grim old man leaned on the fence, and tried to keep back the sobs that shook his bent shoulders. He was half afraid and half ashamed, but there he stood and cried. At last he dried his eyes, and went slowly into the house, as if in hope of comfort as well as shelter.

The two sisters were busy in an upper room. They had seen William Haydon drive away, and their sympathy had been much moved by the sight of his father's grief. They stood at a window watching him from behind the curtain.

"He feels it much as anybody could," said Mrs. Stevens, not without a certain satisfaction in this tribute to her own dear sister. "Somehow or 'nother your brother is so methodical and contained, Mis' Martin, that I shouldn't have looked to see him give way like other men."

"He never was one that could show his feelin's," answered Mrs. Martin. "I never saw him shed tears before as I know of, but many's the time he hasn't been able to control his voice to speak. I wonder what made William hurry off so? His back looked kind o' provoked. They couldn't have had no words; whatever it was, they couldn't had no words so soon as this; an' William 's always respectful."

"'T ain't that either," she added, a moment later. "I've seen sights o' folks in trouble, and I don't know what nor why it is, but they always have to get through with a fractious spell before they can get to work again. They'll hold up an' 'pear splendid, and then something seems to let go, an' everything goes wrong, an' every word plagues 'em. Now Isr'el's my own poor brother, an' you know how I set by him, Mis' Stevens; but I expect we'll have to walk soft to get along with him for a week or two to come. Don't you go an' be too gentle, neither. Treat him just's you would anyway, and he'll fetch himself into line the quicker. He always did have days when he wouldn't say nothing to nobody. It does seem 's if I ought to be the one to stop longer with him, an' be the most help; but you know how I'm situated. And then 't is your sister's things that's to be looked over, and you and Marilla is the proper ones."

"I wish 't was so you could stop," Mrs. Stevens urged honestly. "I feel more acquainted with you than I do with Marilly. But I shall do my best, as I shall want those who come to do for my things when I'm past an' gone. I shall get William to come an' help us; he knows more about his mother's possessions than anybody, I expect. She made a kind of girl of him, for company's sake, when he was little; and he used to sew real pretty before his fingers got too big. Don't you recall one winter when he was house-bound after a run o' scarlet fever? He used to work worsted, and knit some, I believe he did; but he took to growin' that spring, and I chanced to ask him to supply me with a couple o' good holders, but I found I'd touched dignity. He was dreadful put out. I suppose he was mos' too manly for me to refer to his needlework. Poor Marthy! how she laughed! I only said that about the holders for the sake o' sayin' somethin', but he remembered it against me more than a year."

The two aunts laughed together. "Boys is boys, ain't they?" observed Mrs. Stevens, with great sagacity.

"Men is boys," retorted Mrs. Martin. "The more you treat 'em like boys, the better they think you use 'em. They always want motherin', an' somebody to come to. I always tell folks I've got five child'n, counting

Mr. Martin the youngest. The more bluster they have, the more boys they be. Now Marthy knew that about brother Isr'el, an' she always ruled him by love an' easin' of him down from them high perches he was always settin' upon. Everything was always right with her an' all wrong with him when they was young, but she could always say the right word."

"She was a good-feelin' woman; she did make him a good wife, if I say it that shouldn't o' my own sister," sighed Mrs. Stevens. "She was the best o' housekeepers, was Marthy. I never went over so neat a house. I ain't got the gift myself. I can clear up, Mis' Martin, but I can't remain cleared up."

The two sisters turned to their pathetic work of looking over the orderly closets and making solemn researches into the suspected shelters of moths. Much talk of the past was suggested by the folding of blankets; and as they set back the chairs, and brushed the floors that were made untidy by the funeral guests of the day before, they wondered afresh what would become of Israel Haydon, and what plan he would make for himself; for Mrs. Martin could only stay with him for a few days, and Mrs. Stevens was obliged to return as soon as possible to her busy household and an invalid daughter. As long as they could stay the house went on as usual, and Israel Haydon showed no apprehension of difficulties ahead. He took up the routine of his simple fashion of life, and when William asked if he should bring his team to plough, he received the surprised answer that all those things were settled when they talked about them earlier in the spring. Of course he should want potatoes, and it was high time they were planted. A boy arrived from the back country who had lived at the farm the summer before,—a willing, thick-headed young person in process of growth,—and Israel Haydon took great exception to his laziness and inordinate appetite, and threatened so often to send him back where he came from that only William's insistence that they had entered into an engagement with poor Thomas, and the women's efforts toward reconciliation, prevailed.

When sister Martin finally departed, bag and baggage, she felt as if she were leaving her brother to be the prey of disaster. He was sternly self-reliant, and watched her drive away down the lane with something like a sense of relief. The offending Thomas was standing by, expecting rebuke almost with an air of interest; but the old man only said to him, in an apologetic and friendly way, "There! we've got to get along a spell

SARAH ORNE JEWETT

without any women folks, my son. I haven't heard of any housekeeper to suit me, but we'll get along together till I do."

"There's a great sight o' things cooked up, sir," said Thomas, with shining eyes.

"We'll get along," repeated the old man. "I won't have you take no liberties, but if we save the time from other things, we can manage just as well as the women. I want you to sweep out good, night an' morning, an' fetch me the wood an' water, an' I'll see to the housework." There was no idea of appointing Thomas as keeper of the pantry keys, and a shadow of foreboding darkened the lad's hopeful countenance as the master of the house walked away slowly up the yard.

III

It was the month of June; the trees were in full foliage; there was no longer any look of spring in the landscape, and the air and sky belonged to midsummer. Mrs. Israel Haydon had been dead nearly two months.

On a Sunday afternoon the father and son sat in two old splint-bottomed chairs just inside the wood-house, in the shade. The wide doors were always thrown back at that time of the year, and there was a fine view across the country. William Haydon could see his own farm spread out like a green map; he was scanning the boundaries of the orderly fences and fields and the stretches of woodland and pasture. He looked away at them from time to time, or else bent over and poked among the wood-house dust and fine chips with his walking-stick. "There's an old buckle that I lost one day ever so many years ago," he exclaimed suddenly, and reached down to pick it up. William was beginning to look stout and middle-aged. He held out the rusty buckle to his father, but Israel Haydon sat stiffly upright, and hardly gave a glance at the useless object.

"I thought Elder Wall preached an excellent discourse this morning." William made further attempt to engage his father's interest and attention, but without avail.

"I wish you'd tell me what's the matter with you, sir," said the troubled son, turning squarely, and with honest kindness in his look. "It hurts my feelings, father. If I've put you out, I want to make amends. Marilla's worried to death for fear it's on her account. We both set everything by you, but you hold us off; and I feel, when I try to be company for you, as if you thought I belonged in jail, and hadn't no rights of any kind. Can't you talk right out with me, sir? Ain't you well?"

"There! don't run on, boy," said the old man sadly. "I do the best I can; you've got to give me time. I'm dreadful hard pushed losin' of your mother. I've lost my home; you ain't got the least idea what it is, William."

His old face quivered, and William rose hastily and went a step or two forward, making believe that he was looking after his horse. "Stand still, there!" he shouted to the placid creature, and then came back and reached out his hand to his father.

Israel took hold of it, but looked up, a little puzzled. "You ain't going yet?" he asked. "Why, you've only just come."

"I want you to ride over with me to supper to-night. I want you to see how well that piece o' late corn looks, after all your saying I might's well lay it down to turnips. Come, father; the horse's right here, and 't will make a change for you. Ain't you about got through with them pies aunt Martin left you when she went away? Come; we're goin' to have a hearty supper, and I want ye."

"I don't know but I will," said Israel Haydon slowly. "We've got on pretty well—no, we ain't, neither. I ain't comfortable, and I can't make nothin' o' that poor shoat of a boy. I'm buying o' the baker an' frying a pan o' pork the whole time, trying to fill him up. I never was so near out o' pork this time o' year, not since I went to housekeepin'."

"I heard he'd been tellin' round the neighborhood that he was about starved," said William plainly. "Our folks always had the name o' being good providers."

"How'd your mother use to wash up the cups an' things to make 'em look decent?" asked Mr. Haydon suddenly; there was the humility of broken pride in his tone. "I can't seem to find nothin' to do with, anywhere about the house. I s'posed I knew where everything was. I expect I've got out all poor mother's best things, without knowin' the difference. Except there ain't nothin' nowhere that looks right to me," he added.

William stooped to pick something out of the chips. "You'll have to ask Marilla," he said. "It mortifies me to have you go on in such a way. Now, father, you wouldn't hear to anybody that was named to you, but if you go on this way much longer you'll find that any housekeeper's better than none."

"Why, I've only been waiting to hear of a proper person," said Israel Haydon, turning an innocent and aggrieved countenance upon his son. "My house is in a terrible state, now I can tell you."

William looked away and tried to keep his face steady.

"What do you find to laugh at?" asked the poor father, in the tone of a schoolmaster.

"Don't you know I spoke of somebody to you? I believe 't was the very day after the funeral," said William persuasively. "Her name is Maria Durrant."

"I remember the person well; an excellent, sensible woman, no flummery, and did remarkable well in case of sickness at your house," said Mr. Haydon, with enthusiasm, stepping briskly toward the wagon after he had shut and fastened the wood-house doors and put the padlock key in his pocket. "What of her? You said there was no chance of getting her, didn't you?"

"I was afraid so; but she's left her brother's folks now, and come to stop a little while with Marilla. She's at the house this minute; came last night. You know, Marilla's very fond of having her cousins come to stop with her," apologized the son, in fear lest his simple plot should be discovered and resented. "You can see if she's such a person as you want. I have been thinking all day that she might do for a time, anyway."

"Anybody'll do," said Mr. Haydon suddenly. "I tell ye, William, I'm drove to the wall. I feel to covet a good supper; an' I'm ashamed to own it, a man o' my property! I'll observe this Miss Durrant, an' speak with her after tea; perhaps she'd have the sense to come right over to-morrow. You an' Marilla can tell her how I've been situated. I wa'n't going to have no such persons in my house as were recommended," he grumbled on cheerfully. "I don't keep a town-farm for the incapable, nor do I want an old grenadier set over me like that old maid Smith. I ain't going to be turned out of my own house."

They drove along the road slowly, and presently the ever-interesting subject of crops engaged their further attention. When they turned into William Haydon's side yard a pleasant-faced, middle-aged woman, in a neat black dress and a big clean white apron, sat on the piazza with Marilla and the children. Israel Haydon's heart felt lighter than it had for many a week. He went and shook hands with Maria Durrant, with more than interest and approval; there was even a touch of something like gallantry in his manner. William Haydon glanced at his wife and gave an unconscious sigh of relief.

The next morning Miss Durrant helped with the early work, talking with William's wife as she went to and fro busily in the large kitchen, and listening to all that could be said of the desperate state of affairs at the old farm. The two women so doubled their diligence by working together that it was still early in the day when Maria, blushing noticeably, said that she thought there was no use in waiting until afternoon, as old Mr. Haydon had directed. There must be plenty to do; and the sooner the house was put to rights and some cooking got under way the better. She had her old calico dress all on, and she deemed it best to go over and go right to work.

"There! I don't know what to say, Maria," said Marilla Haydon doubtfully. "Father Haydon's such a set person."

"So be I," rejoined Maria. "And who knows how bad those rooms need airing! I've thought of twenty things that ought to be done right off, before night. Or I could work a spell in the gardin if he don't seem to want me in the house. Now, wa'n't it affectin' to hear him let on that he'd gone an' made poor Mis' Haydon's flower gardin same's he'd always done? It showed real feelin', didn't it? I am goin' to take holt over there as if 't was for her as well as for him. That time I was here so long, when you was so sick, I did just admire Mis' Haydon. She was a beautiful-looking woman, and so pretty-behaved; quiet, but observin'. I never saw a man age as William's father has; it made my heart ache when I first caught sight of him driving into the yard last night."

"He revived up conversin' with you an' makin' such a good hearty tea," suggested Marilla, disappearing in the pantry. "I ain't never felt free with father Haydon, but I do respect him," she added presently. "Well, now, go right over, Maria, if you feel moved to. I don't know but what you're wise. P'r'aps William an' I'll walk over, after supper's put away. I guess you've got a busy day before you."

She stood at the open door and watched Maria Durrant go away, a few minutes later, with a plump bundle under one arm.

"I should think you were going to seek your fortune," she called merrily, as the good woman turned into the road; but Maria wagged her head with a cheerful nod, and did not deign to look back. "I ought to have given her some bread to tuck under the other arm, like the picture of Benjamin Franklin. I dare say they do need bread; I ought to have thought of it," said Marilla anxiously, as she returned to the pantry.

"But there! Father Haydon's got as far along in housekeeping as stopping the baker; an' he was put out because I sent things too soon, before aunt Martin's provisions were gone. I'll risk cousin Maria to get along."

The new housekeeper trod the little footpath at the road edge with a firm step. She was as eager and delighted as if she were bent on a day's pleasuring. A truly sympathetic, unselfish heart beat in her breast; she fairly longed to make the lonely, obstinate old man comfortable. Presently she found herself going up the long Haydon lane in the shade of the apple-trees. The great walnut-trees at the other side of the house were huge and heavy with leaves; there was a general floweriness and pleasantness over all growing things; but the tall thin spruce that towered before the front door looked black and solitary, and bore a likeness to old Mr. Haydon himself. Such was the force of this comparison that Miss Durrant stopped and looked at it with compassion.

Then her eyes fell upon the poor flower bed overgrown with weeds, through which the bachelor's-buttons and London-pride were pushing their way into bloom. "I guess I'll set a vine to grow up that tree; 't would get sun enough, an' look real live and pretty," she decided, surveying the situation; then she moved on, with perhaps less eagerness in her gait, and boldly entered the side door of the house. She could hear the sound of an axe in the shed, as if some one were chopping up kindlings. When she caught sight of the empty kitchen she dropped her bundle into the nearest chair, and held up her hands in what was no affectation of an appearance of despair.

IV

One day in May, about a year from the time that Martha Haydon died, Maria Durrant was sitting by the western window of the kitchen, mending Mr. Haydon's second-best black coat, when she looked down the lane and saw old Polly Norris approaching the house. Polly was an improvident mother of improvident children, not always quite sound in either wits or behavior, but she had always been gently dealt with by the Haydons, and, as it happened, was also an old acquaintance of Maria Durrant's own. Maria gave a little groan at the sight of her: she did not feel just then like listening to long tales or responding to troublesome demands. She nodded kindly to the foolish old creature, who presently came wheezing and lamenting into the clean sunshiny kitchen, and dropped herself like an armful of old clothes into the nearest chair.

Maria rose and put by her work; she was half glad, after all, to have company; and Polly Norris was not without certain powers of good-fellowship and entertaining speech.

"I expect this may be the last time I can get so fur," she announced. "'T is just 'bout a year sence we was all to Mis' Haydon's funeral. I didn't know but that was the last time. Well, I do' know but it's so I can accept that piece o' pie. I've come fur, an' my strength's but small. How's William's folks?"

"They're smart," answered Maria, seating herself to her work again, after the expedition to the pantry.

"I tell ye this is beautiful pie," said the guest, looking up, after a brief and busy silence; "a real comfortable help o' pie, after such a walk, feeble as I be. I've failed a sight sence you see me before, now ain't I?"

"I don't know's I see any change to speak of," said Maria, bending over the coat.

"Lord bless you, an' Heaven too! I ain't eat no such pie as this sence I was a girl. Your rule, was it, or poor Mis' Haydon's?"

"I've always made my pies that same way," said Maria soberly. "I'm pleased you should enjoy it."

"I expect my walk give me an extry appetite. I can walk like a bird, now, I tell ye; last summer I went eleven miles, an' ag'in nine miles. You just ought to see me on the road, an' here I be, goin' on seventy-seven year old. There ain't so many places to go to as there used to be. I've known a sight o' nice kind folks that's all gone. It's re'lly sad how folks is goin'. There's all Mis' Nash's folks passed away; the old doctor, an' the little grandgirl, an' Mis' Nash that was like a mother to me, an' always had some thin' to give me; an' down to Glover's Corner they're all gone"—

"Yes, anybody feels such changes," replied Maria compassionately. "You've seen trouble, ain't you?"

"I've seen all kinds of trouble," said the withered little creature, mournfully.

"How is your daughter to South Atfield gettin' along?" asked the hostess kindly, after a pause, while Polly worked away at the pie.

"Lord bless you! this pie is so heartenin', somehow or 'nother, after such a walk. Susan Louisa is doin' pretty well; she's a sight improved from what she was. Folks is very considerate to Susan Louisa. She goes to the Orthodox church, an' sence she was sick there's been a committee to see to her. They met, fifteen in number. One on 'em give her two quarts o' milk a day. Mr. Dean, Susan Louisa's husband, died the eighth day o' last March."

"Yes, I heard he was gone, rather sudden," said Maria, showing more interest.

"Yes, but he was 'twixt eighty an' ninety year old. Susan Louisa was but fifty-one in February last."

"He'd have done better for you, wouldn't he, Mis' Norris?" suggested Maria, by way of pleasantry, but there was a long and doubtful pause.

"I had rather be excused," said Polly at last, with great emphasis. "Miss Maria Durrant, ain't you got a calico dress you could spare, or an apron, or a pair o' rubbers, anyways? I be extra needy, now, I tell you! There; I ain't inquired for William's folks; how be they?"

"All smart," said Maria, for the second time; but she happened to look up just in time to catch a strange gleam in her visitor's eyes.

"Mis' William don't come here, I expect?" she asked mysteriously.

"She never was no great of a visitor. Yes, she comes sometimes," answered Maria Durrant.

"I understood William had forbid her till you'd got away, if she was your own cousin."

"We're havin' no trouble together. What do you mean?" Maria demanded.

"Well, my hearing ain't good." Polly tried to get herself into safe shelter of generalities. "Old folks kind o' dreams things; you must excuse me, Maria. But I certain have heard a sight o' talk about your stoppin' here so long with Mr. Haydon, and that William thought you was overdoin', an' would have spoke, only you was his wife's cousin. There's plenty stands up for you; I should always be one of 'em my self; you needn't think but I'm a friend, Maria. I heard somebody a-remarking that you was goin' to stay till you got him; an' others said Mr. Israel Haydon was one to know his own mind, and he never would want to put nobody in his wife's place, they set so by one another. An' I spoke a good word for ye. I says, 'Now look here! 't ain't 's if Mari' Durrant was a girl o' twenty-five; she's a smart capable creatur',' says I, 'an'"—

"I guess I've got an old dress I can let you have."

Maria Durrant, with crimson cheeks and a beating heart, rose suddenly and escaped to the back stairway. She left old Polly sitting in the kitchen so long that she fell into a comfortable drowse, from which she was recalled by Maria's reappearance with a bundle of discarded garments, but there was something stern and inhospitable in these last moments of the visit, and Polly soon shuffled off down the lane, mumbling and muttering and hugging the bundle with great delight. She always enjoyed her visits to the Haydon farm. But she had left Miss Durrant crying by the western window; the bitter tears were falling on Israel Haydon's old black coat. It seemed very hard that a woman who had spent all her life working for others should be treated as the enemy of kindred and acquaintance; this was almost the first time in all her history that she had managed to gather and hold a little peace and happiness. There was nothing to do now but to go back to her brother's noisy shiftless house; to work against wind and tide of laziness and improvidence. She must slave for the three boarders, so that her brother's wife could go to New York State to waste her time with a sister just as worthless, though not so penniless, as herself. And there was young Johnny, her nephew, working with Mr. Haydon on the farm, and doing so well, he must go back too, and be put into the factory. Maria looked out of the window; through the tears that stood in her eyes the smooth green fields were magnified and transfigured.

The door opened, and Mr. Haydon entered with deliberate step and a pleasant reassuring look. He almost never smiled, but he happened to be smiling then. "I observed you had company just now; I saw old Polly Norris going down the lane when I was coming up from the field," he said, and then stopped suddenly, and took a step nearer to Maria; he had never seen his cheerful housemate in tears. He did not ask the reason; they both felt embarrassed, and yet each was glad of the other's presence.

Mr. Haydon did not speak, but Maria brushed her tears away, and tried to go on sewing. She was mending the lining of the second-best black coat with most touching care.

"I expect I shall have to take that co't for every day now, an' get me a new one for best," he announced at last, because somebody had to say something. "I've about finished with this. Spring work is hard on an old co't."

"Your best one is gettin' a little mite threadbare in the back," said Maria, but it was hard for her to control her voice. "I'll put all your clothes in as good repair as I can before I go, sir. I've come to the conclusion that I ought to go back to my brother's folks, his wife wants to go off on a visit"—

"Don't you, Maria," exclaimed the distressed old man. "Don't talk that way; it's onreasonable. William has informed me about your brother's folks; what else may affect you I don't know, but I've made up my mind. I don't know why 't was, but I was just comin' to speak about it. I may say 't was for your interest as well as mine, an' with William's approval. I never thought to change my situation till lately. Such a loss as I've met ain't to be forgotten, an' it ain't forgotten. I'm gettin' along in years, an' I never was a great talker. I expect you know what I want to say, Miss Durrant. I'll provide well for you, an' make such a settlement as you an' William approve. He's well off, an' he spoke to me about us; that we was comfortable together, an' he never wanted to see me left alone, as I was last year. How do you feel yourself? You feel that 't would be good judgment, now don't ye?"

Maria never had heard Mr. Israel Haydon say so much at any one time. There he stood, a man of sixty-eight, without pretense of having fallen in love, but kind and just, and almost ministerial in his respectability. She had always followed a faint but steady star of romance, which shone still for her in the lowering sky of her life; it seemed to shine before her eyes now; it dazzled her through fresh tears. Yet, after all, she felt that this was really her home, and with a sudden great beat of her heart, she knew that she should say "Yes" to Mr. Haydon. The sharp sting in the thought of going away had been that she must leave him to the ignorant devotion or neglect of somebody else—some other woman was going to have the dear delight of making him comfortable.

So she looked up full in his face, unmindful of the bleakness of his love-making, and was touched to see that he bore the aspect of a truly anxious and even affectionate man. Without further words they both knew that the great question was settled. The star of romance presently turned itself into the bright kitchen lamp that stood between them as Maria sewed her long winter seam and looked up contentedly to see Mr. Haydon sitting opposite with his weekly newspaper.

V

Mr. Haydon owned one of the last old-fashioned two-wheeled chaises, a select few of which still survived in the retired region of Atfield. It would not have suited him to go to church in a wagon like his neighbors, any more than he could have bought a rough working-suit of new clothes for every day. The chaise-top had always framed the faces of Mr. Haydon and Martha, his first wife, in a fitting manner not unlike a Friend's plain bonnet on a larger scale; it had belonged to their placid appearance of old-time respectability. Now that Maria, the second wife, had taken the vacant seat by the driver's side, her fresher color and eager enjoyment of the comfort and dignity of the situation were remarked with pleasure. She had not been forward about keeping Mr. Haydon company before their marriage; for some reason she was not a constant church-goer, and usually had some excuse for staying at home, both on Sundays and when there was any expedition on business to one of the neighboring towns. But after the wedding these invitations were accepted as a matter of course.

One Sunday afternoon they were bobbing home from meeting in their usual sedate and placid fashion. There had been a very good sermon, and two or three strangers in the congregation, old acquaintances who had left Atfield for the West, stopped to speak with their friends after the service was over. It was a lovely day, and there was the peacefulness of Sunday over the landscape, the wide untenanted fields, the woods near and far, and the distant hills. The old pacing horse jogged steadily along.

"I was thinking how your wife would have enjoyed seeing the folks; wouldn't she?" said Maria, with gentle sympathy.

"The thought was just dwelling in my mind," said the old man, turning toward her, a little surprised.

"I was sorry I was stand in' right there; they didn't feel so free to speak, you know," said Maria, who had accepted her place as substitute with a touching self-forgetfulness and devotion, following as best she could the humblest by-paths of the first Mrs. Haydon's career.

"Marthy and Mis' Chellis that you saw to-day was always the best of friends; they was girls together," said Mr. Haydon, swaying his whip-lash. "They was second cousins on the father's side."

"Don't you expect Mis' Chellis'd like to come an' take tea with you some afternoon? I always feel as if 't would be sad for you, such an occasion, but I'll have everything real nice. Folks seem to be paying her a good deal of attention," suggested Maria.

"And when anybody has been away a good while, they like to go all round and see all the places that's familiar, if they do feel the changes."

"Yes, I guess we'd better invite her to spend the afternoon," said the old man, and they jogged on together in silence.

"Have you got everything you want to do with?", asked Mr. Haydon kindly.

"Certain," answered Maria, with satisfaction. "I never was acquainted with such a good provider as you be in all the houses I've ever stopped in; I can say that. You've remembered a number o' things this past week that I should have forgot myself. I've seen what other women folks has to go through with, being obliged to screw every way an' make up things out o' nothing, afraid to say the flour's gone or the sugar's out. Them very husbands is the ones that'll find most fault if their tables ain't spread with what they want. I know now what made your wife always look so pleased an' contented."

"She was very saving an' judicious by natur'," said Mr. Haydon, as if he did not wish to take so much praise entirely to himself. "I call you a very saving woman too, Maria," he added, looking away over the fields, as if he had made some remark about the grass.

The bright color rushed to Maria's face, but she could not say anything. There was something very pleasant in the air; the fields appeared new to her and most beautiful; it was a moment of great happiness.

"I tell you I felt it dreadfully when I was alone all that time. I enjoy having somebody to speak with now about poor Martha," said the old man, with great feeling.

"It was dreadful lonely for you, wa'n't it?" said Maria, in her sensible, pleasant, compassionate tone.

"People meant well enough with their advice, but I was set so cross-wise that it all seemed like interference. I'd got to wait till the right thing came round—an' it come at last," announced Mr. Haydon handsomely. "I feel to be very grateful. Yes, I want to have Mis' Chellis come an' take tea, just as she used to. We'll look over what's left o' poor Marthy's little things, an' select something to give her for a remembrance. 'T ain't very likely she'll come 'way East again at her time o' life. She's havin' a grand time; it acts to me just like a last visit."

"I'll make some nice pound-cake to-morrow, and we'll ask her next day," said Maria cheerfully, as they turned into the lane.

Maria Haydon's life had been spent in trying to make other people comfortable, and so she succeeded, oftener than she knew, in making them happy. Every day she seemed to forget herself, and to think of others more; and so, though old Mrs. Chellis missed her friend when she came to tea the next day but one, she soon forgot the sadness of the first few minutes, and began to enjoy the kind welcome of Mr. Haydon and his present companion.

A little later Mr. Haydon was coming back from one of his fields to look after some men whom he and his son had set to work at ditching. Most of the talk that afternoon had naturally been connected with his first wife, but now everything along his path reminded him of Maria. Her prosperous flock of young turkeys were heading northward at a little distance out across the high grass land; and below, along the brook, went the geese and goslings in a sedate procession. The young pear-trees which she had urged him to set out looked thrifty and strong as he passed, and there were some lengths of linen bleaching on a knoll, that she had found yellowing in one of the garret chests. She took care of everything, and, best of all, she took great care of him. He had left the good creature devoting herself to their guest as if she were an old friend instead of a stranger—just for his sake and his wife's sake. Maria always said "your wife" when she spoke of her predecessor.

"Marthy always said that Maria Durrant was as kind and capable a woman as she ever set eyes on, an' poor Marthy was one that knew," said Mr. Haydon to himself as he went along, and his heart grew very tender. He was not exactly satisfied with himself, but he could not have told why. As he came near, the house looked cheerful and pleasant; the front door was wide open, and the best-room blinds. The little garden was in full bloom, and there was a sound of friendly voices. Conversation was flowing on with a deep and steady current. Somehow the old man felt young again in the midst of his sober satisfaction and renewed prosperity. He lingered near the door, and looked back over his fields as if he were facing life with a sense of great security; but presently his ears caught at something that the two women were saying in the house.

Maria was speaking to Mrs. Chellis, who was a little deaf.

"Yes'm, he does look well," she said. "I think his health's a good sight better than it was a year ago. I don't know's you ever saw anybody so pitiful as he was for a good while after he lost his wife. He took it harder than some o' those do that make more talk. Yes, she certain was a lovely woman, and one that knew how to take the lead for him just where a man don't want to be bothered—about house matters and little things. He's a dear, good, kind man, Mr. Haydon is. I feel very grateful for all his kindness. I've got a lovely home, Mis' Chellis," said Maria impulsively; "an' I try to do everything I can, the way he an' Mis' Haydon always had it."

"I guess you do," agreed the guest. "I never see him look better since he was a young man. I hope he knows how well off he is!"

They both laughed a little, and Mr. Haydon could not help smiling in sympathy.

"There, I do enjoy spending with him," said the younger woman wistfully; "but I can't help wishin' sometimes that I could have been the one to help him save. I envy Mis' Haydon all that part of it, and I can't help it."

"Why, you must set a sight by him!" exclaimed Mrs. Chellis, with mild surprise. "I didn't know but what marryin' for love had all gone out of fashion in Atfield."

"You can tell 'em it ain't," said Maria. At that moment Israel Haydon turned and walked away slowly up the yard. His thin black figure straightened itself gallantly, and he wore the look of a younger man.

Later that evening, when the guests were gone, after a most cheerful and hospitable occasion, and the company tea things were all put away, Maria was sitting in the kitchen for a few minutes to rest, and Mr. Haydon had taken his own old chair near the stove, and sat there tapping his finger-ends together. They had congratulated each other handsomely, because everything had gone off so well; but suddenly they both felt as if there were a third person present; their feeling toward one another seemed to change. Something seemed to prompt them to new confidence and affection, to speak the affectionate thoughts that were in their hearts; it was no rebuking, injured presence, for a sense of great contentment filled their minds. Israel Haydon tapped his fingers less regularly than usual, and Maria found herself unable to meet his eyes.

The silence between them grew more and more embarrassing, and at last Mr. Haydon remembered that he had not locked the barn, and rose at once, crossing the kitchen with quicker steps than usual. Maria looked up at him as he passed.

"Yes, everything went off beautifully," she repeated. "Mis' Chellis is real good company. I enjoyed hearing her talk about old times. She set everything by Mis' Haydon, didn't she? You had a good wife,

Mr. Haydon, certain," said Maria, wistfully, as he hesitated a moment at the door.

Israel Haydon did not answer a word, but went his way and shut the door behind him. It was a cool evening after the pleasant day; the air felt a little chilly. He did not go beyond the doorsteps, for something seemed to draw him back, so he lifted the clinking latch and stepped bravely into the kitchen again, and stood there a moment in the bright light.

Maria Haydon turned toward him as she stood at the cupboard with a little lamp in her hand. "Why Mr. Haydon! what's the matter?" She looked startled at first, but her face began to shine. "Now don't you go and be foolish, Isr'el!" she said.

"Maria," said he, "I want to say to you that I feel to be very thankful. I've got a good wife *now*."

LITTLE FRENCH MARY

The town of Dulham was not used to seeing foreigners of any sort, or to hearing their voices in its streets, so that it was in some sense a matter of public interest when a Canadian family was reported to have come to the white house by the bridge. This house, small and low-storied, with a bushy little garden in front, had been standing empty for several months. Usually when a house was left tenantless in Dulham it remained so and fell into decay, and, after some years, the cinnamon rose bushes straggled into the cellar, and the dutiful grass grew over the mound that covered the chimney bricks. Dulham was a quiet place, where the population dwindled steadily, though such citizens as remained had reason to think it as pleasant as any country town in the world.

Some of the old men who met every day to talk over the town affairs were much interested in the newcomers. They approved the course of the strong-looking young Canadian laborer who had been quick to seize upon his opportunity; one or two of them had already engaged him to make their gardens, and to do odd jobs, and were pleased with his quickness and willingness. He had come afoot one day from a neighboring town, where he and his wife had been made ill by bad drainage and factory work, and saw the little house, and asked the postmaster if there were any work to be had out of doors that spring in Dulham. Being assured of his prospects, he reappeared with his pale, bright-eyed wife and little daughter the very next day but one. This startling promptness had given time for but few persons to hear the news of a new neighbor, and as one after another came over the bridge and along the road there were many questions asked. The house seemed to have new life looking out of its small-paned windows; there were clean white curtains, and china dogs on the window-sills, and a blue smoke in the chimney—the spring sun was shining in at the wide-open door.

There was a chilly east wind on an April day, and the elderly men were gathered inside the post-office, which was also the chief grocery and dry-goods store. Each was in his favorite armchair, and there was the excuse of a morning fire in the box stove to make them form again into the close group that was usually broken up at the approach of summer weather. Old Captain Weathers was talking about Alexis, the newcomer (they did not try to pronounce his last name), and was saying for the third or fourth time that the more work you set for the Frenchman the better pleased he seemed to be. "Helped 'em to lay a carpet yesterday at our house, neat as wax," said the Captain, with approval. "Made the garden in the front yard so it hasn't looked so well for years. We're all goin' to find him very handy; he'll have plenty to do among us all summer. Seems to know what you want the minute you p'int, for he can't make out very well with his English. I used to be able to talk considerable French in my early days when I sailed from southern ports to Havre and Bordeaux, but I don't seem to recall it now very well. He'd have made a smart sailor, Alexis would; quick an' willing."

"They say Canada French ain't spoken the same, anyway"—began the Captain's devoted friend, Mr. Ezra Spooner, by way of assurance, when the store door opened and a bright little figure stood looking in. All the gray-headed men turned that way, and every one of them smiled.

"Come right in, dear," said the kind-hearted old Captain.

They saw a charming little creature about six years old, who smiled back again from under her neat bit of a hat; she wore a pink frock that made her look still more like a flower, and she said "*Bonjour*" prettily to the gentlemen as she passed. Henry Staples, the storekeeper and postmaster, rose behind the counter to serve this customer as if she had been a queen, and took from her hand the letter she brought, with the amount of its postage folded up in a warm bit of newspaper.

The Captain and his friends looked on with admiration.

"Give her a piece of candy—no, give it to me an' I'll give it to her," said the Captain eagerly, reaching for his cane and leaving his chair with more than usual agility; and everybody looked on with intent while he took a striped stick of peppermint from the storekeeper and offered it gallantly. There was something in the way this favor was accepted that savored of the French court and made every man in the store a lover.

The child made a quaint bow before she reached out her hand with childish eagerness for the unexpected delight; then she stepped forward and kissed the Captain.

There was a murmur of delight at this charming courtesy; there was not a man who would not have liked to find some excuse for walking away with her, and there was a general sigh as she shut the door behind her and looked back through the glass with a parting smile.

"That's little French Mary, Alexis's little girl," said the storekeeper, eager to proclaim his advantage of previous acquaintance. "She came here yesterday and did an errand for her mother as nice as a grown person could."

"I never saw a little creatur' with prettier ways," said the Captain, blushing and tapping his cane on the floor.

SARAH ORNE JEWETT

This first appearance of the little foreigner on an April day was like the coming of a young queen to her kingdom. She reigned all summer over every heart in Dulham—there was not a face but wore its smiles when French Mary came down the street, not a mother who did not say to her children that she wished they had such pretty manners and kept their frocks as neat. The child danced and sang like a fairy, and condescended to all childish games, and yet, best of all for her friends, she seemed to see no difference between young and old. She sometimes followed Captain Weathers home, and discreetly dined or took tea with him and his housekeeper, an honored guest; on rainy days she might be found in the shoemaker's shop or the blacksmith's, as still as a mouse, and with eyes as bright and quick, watching them at their work; smiling much but speaking little, and teaching as much French as she learned English. To this day, in Dulham, people laugh and repeat her strange foreign words and phrases. Alexis, the father, was steady at his work of gardening and haying; Marie, the elder, his wife, washed and ironed and sewed and swept, and was a helper in many households; now and then on Sunday they set off early in the morning and walked to the manufacturing town whence they had come, to go to mass; at the end of the summer, when they felt prosperous, they sometimes hired a horse and wagon, and drove there with the child between them. Dulham village was the brighter and better for their presence, and the few old-fashioned houses that knew them treasured them, and French Mary reigned over her kingdom with no revolt or disaffection to the summer's end. She seemed to fulfill all the duties of her childish life by some exquisite instinct and infallible sense of fitness and propriety.

One September morning, after the first frost, the Captain and his friends were sitting in the store with the door shut. The Captain was the last comer.

"I've got bad news," he said, and they all turned toward him, apprehensive and forewarned.

"Alexis says he's going right away" (regret was mingled with the joy of having a piece of news to tell). "Yes, Alexis is going away; he's packing up now, and has spoke for Foster's hay-cart to move his stuff to the railroad."

"What makes him so foolish?" said Mr. Spooner.

"He says his folks expect him in Canada; he's got an aunt livin' there that owns a good house and farm, and she's gettin' old and wants to have him settled at home to take care of her."

"I've heard these French folks only desire to get forehanded a little, and then they go right back where they come from," said some one, with an air of disapproval.

"He says he'll send another man here; he knows somebody that will be glad of the chance, but I don't seem to like the idea so well," said Captain Weathers doubtfully. "We've all got so used to Alexis and his wife; they know now where we keep every thing and have got to be so handy. Strange they don't know when they're well off. I suppose it's natural they should want to be with their own folks. Then there's the little girl."

At this moment the store door was opened and French Mary came in. She was dressed in her best and her eyes were shining.

"I go to Canada in ze cars!" she announced joyfully, and came dancing down between the two long counters toward her regretful friends; they had never seen her so charming.

Argument and regret were impossible—the forebodings of elderly men and their experience of life were of no use at that moment, a gleam of youth and hope was theirs by sympathy instead. A child's pleasure in a journey moves the dullest heart; the captain was the first to find some means of expression.

"Give me some o' that best candy for her," he commanded the storekeeper. "No, take a bigger piece of paper, and tie it up well."

"Ain't she dressed a little thin for travelin'?" asked gruff Mr. Spooner anxiously, and for his part he pointed the storekeeper to a small bright plaid shawl that hung overhead, and stooped to wrap it himself about the little shoulders.

"I must get the little girl something, too," said the minister, who was a grandfather, and had just come in for his mail. "What do you like best, my dear?" and French Mary pointed shyly, but with instant decision, at a blue silk parasol, with a white handle, which was somewhat the worse for having been openly displayed all summer. The minister bought it with pleasure, like a country boy at a fair, and put into her hand.

French Mary kissed the minister with rapture, and gave him her hand to shake, then she put down the parasol and ran and climbed into the old captain's lap and hugged him with both arms tight round his neck. She considered for a moment whether she should kiss Mr. Ezra Spooner or not, but happily did not decide against it, and said an affectionate good-by to him and all the rest. Mr. Staples himself came out from behind the counter to say farewell and bestow a square package of raisins. They all followed her to the door, and stood watching while she tucked her bundles under her arm and raised the new parasol, and walked away down the street in the chilly autumn morning. She had taken all her French gayety and charm, all her childish sweetness and dignity away with her. Little French Mary had gone. Fate had plucked her like a flower out of their lives.

She did not turn back, but when she was half-way home she began to run, and the new shawl was given gayly to the breeze. The captain sighed.

"I wish the little girl well," he said, and turned away. "We shall miss her, but she doesn't know what parting is. I hope she'll please 'em just as well in Canada."

THE GUESTS OF MRS. TIMMS

I

Mrs. Persis Flagg stood in her front doorway taking leave of Miss Cynthia Pickett, who had been making a long call. They were not intimate friends. Miss Pickett always came formally to the front door and rang when she paid her visits, but, the week before, they had met at the county conference, and happened to be sent to the same house for entertainment, and so had deepened and renewed the pleasures of acquaintance.

It was an afternoon in early June; the syringa-bushes were tall and green on each side of the stone doorsteps, and were covered with their lovely white and golden flowers. Miss Pickett broke off the nearest twig, and held it before her prim face as she talked. She had a pretty childlike smile that came and went suddenly, but her face was not one that bore the marks of many pleasures. Mrs. Flagg was a tall, commanding sort of person, with an air of satisfaction and authority.

"Oh, yes, gather all you want," she said stiffly, as Miss Pickett took the syringa without having asked beforehand; but she had an amiable expression, and just now her large countenance was lighted up by pleasant anticipation.

"We can tell early what sort of a day it's goin' to be," she said eagerly. "There ain't a cloud in the sky now. I'll stop for you as I come along, or if there should be anything unforeseen to detain me, I'll send you word. I don't expect you'd want to go if it wa'n't so that I could?"

"Oh my sakes, no!" answered Miss Pickett discreetly, with a timid flush. "You feel certain that Mis' Timms won't be put out? I shouldn't feel free to go unless I went 'long o' you."

"Why, nothin' could be plainer than her words," said Mrs. Flagg in a tone of reproval. "You saw how she urged me, an' had over all that talk about how we used to see each other often when we both lived to Longport, and told how she'd been thinkin' of writin', and askin' if it wa'n't so I should be able to come over and stop three or four days as soon as settled weather come, because she couldn't make no fire in her best chamber on account of the chimbley smokin' if the wind wa'n't just right. You see how she felt toward me, kissin' of me comin' and goin'? Why, she even asked me who I employed to do over my bonnet, Miss Pickett, just as interested as if she was a sister; an' she remarked she should look for us any pleasant day after we all got home, an' were settled after the conference."

Miss Pickett smiled, but did not speak, as if she expected more arguments still.

"An' she seemed just about as much gratified to meet with you again. She seemed to desire to meet you again very particular," continued Mrs. Flagg. "She really urged us to come together an' have a real good day talkin' over old times—there, don't le' 's go all over it again! I've always heard she'd made that old house of her aunt Bascoms' where she lives look real handsome. I once heard her best parlor carpet described as being an elegant carpet, different from any there was round here. Why, nobody couldn't be more cordial, Miss Pickett; you ain't goin' to give out just at the last?"

"Oh, no!" answered the visitor hastily; "no, 'm! I want to go full as much as you do, Mis' Flagg, but you see I never was so well acquainted with Mis' Cap'n Timms, an' I always seem to dread putting myself for'ard. She certain was very urgent, an' she said plain enough to come any day next week, an' here 'tis Wednesday, though of course she wouldn't look for us either Monday or Tuesday. 'T will be a real pleasant occasion, an' now we've been to the conference it don't seem near so much effort to start."

"Why, I don't think nothin' of it," said Mrs. Flagg proudly. "We shall have a grand good time, goin' together an' all, I feel sure."

Miss Pickett still played with her syringa flower, tapping her thin cheek, and twirling the stem with her fingers. She looked as if she were going to say something more, but after a moment's hesitation she turned away.

"Good-afternoon, Mis' Flagg," she said formally, looking up with a quick little smile; "I enjoyed my call; I hope I ain't kep' you too late; I don't know but what it's 'most tea-tune. Well, I shall look for you in the mornin'."

"Good-afternoon, Miss Pickett; I'm glad I was in when you came. Call again, won't you?" said Mrs. Flagg. "Yes; you may expect me in good season," and so they parted. Miss Pickett went out at the neat clicking gate in the white fence, and Mrs. Flagg a moment later looked out of her sitting-room window to see if the gate were latched, and felt the least bit disappointed to find that it was. She sometimes went out after the departure of a guest, and fastened the gate herself with a loud, rebuking sound. Both of these Woodville women lived alone, and were very precise in their way of doing things.

SARAH ORNE JEWETT

II

The next morning dawned clear and bright, and Miss Pickett rose even earlier than usual. She found it most difficult to decide which of her dresses would be best to wear. Summer was still so young that the day had all the freshness of spring, but when the two friends walked away together along the shady street, with a chorus of golden robins singing high overhead in the elms, Miss Pickett decided that she had made a wise choice of her second-best black silk gown, which she had just turned again and freshened. It was neither too warm for the season nor too cool, nor did it look overdressed. She wore her large cameo pin, and this, with a long watch-chain, gave an air of proper mural decoration. She was a straight, flat little person, as if, when not in use, she kept herself, silk dress and all, between the leaves of a book. She carried a noticeable parasol with a fringe, and a small shawl, with a pretty border, neatly folded over her left arm. Mrs. Flagg always dressed in black cashmere, and looked, to hasty observers, much the same one day as another; but her companion recognized the fact that this was the best black cashmere of all, and for a moment quailed at the thought that Mrs. Flagg was paying such extreme deference to their prospective hostess. The visit turned for a moment into an unexpectedly solemn formality, and pleasure seemed to wane before Cynthia Pickett's eyes, yet with great courage she never slackened a single step. Mrs. Flagg carried a somewhat worn black leather hand-bag, which Miss Pickett regretted; it did not give the visit that casual and unpremeditated air which she felt to be more elegant.

"Sha'n't I carry your bag for you?" she asked timidly. Mrs. Flagg was the older and more important person.

"Oh, dear me, no," answered Mrs. Flagg. "My pocket's so remote, in case I should desire to sneeze or anything, that I thought 't would be convenient for carrying my handkerchief and pocket-book; an' then I just tucked in a couple o' glasses o' my crab-apple jelly for Mis' Timms. She used to be a great hand for preserves of every sort, an' I thought 't would be a kind of an attention, an' give rise to conversation. I know she used to make excellent drop-cakes when we was both residin' to Longport; folks used to say she never would give the right receipt, but if I get a real good chance, I mean to ask her. Or why can't you, if I start talkin' about receipts—why can't you say, sort of innocent, that I have always spoken frequently of her drop-cakes, an' ask for the rule? She would be very sensible to the compliment, and could pass it off if she didn't feel to indulge us. There, I do so wish you would!"

"Yes, 'm," said Miss Pickett doubtfully; "I'll try to make the opportunity. I'm very partial to drop-cakes. Was they flour or rye, Mis' Flagg?"

"They was flour, dear," replied Mrs. Flagg approvingly; "crisp an' light as any you ever see."

"I wish I had thought to carry somethin' to make it pleasant," said Miss Pickett, after they had walked a little farther; "but there, I don't know's 't would look just right, this first visit, to offer anything to such a person as Mis' Timms. In case I ever go over to Baxter again I won't forget to make her some little present, as nice as I've got. 'T was certain very polite of her to urge me to come with you. I did feel very doubtful at first. I didn't know but she thought it behooved her, because I was in your company at the conference, and she wanted to save my feelin's, and yet expected I would decline. I never was well acquainted with her; our folks wasn't well off when I first knew her; 't was before uncle Cap'n Dyer passed away an' remembered mother an' me in his will. We couldn't make no han'some companies in them days, so we didn't go to none, an' kep' to ourselves; but in my grandmother's time, mother always said, the families was very friendly. I shouldn't feel like goin' over to pass the day with Mis' Timms if I didn't mean to ask her to return the visit. Some don't think o' these things, but mother was very set about not bein' done for when she couldn't make no return."

"'When it rains porridge hold up your dish,'" said Mrs. Flagg; but Miss Pickett made no response beyond a feeble "Yes, 'm," which somehow got caught in her pale-green bonnet-strings.

"There, 't ain't no use to fuss too much over all them things," proclaimed Mrs. Flagg, walking along at a good pace with a fine sway of her skirts, and carrying her head high. "Folks walks right by an' forgits all about you; folks can't always be going through with just so much. You'd had a good deal better time, you an' your ma, if you'd been freer in your ways; now don't you s'pose you would? 'T ain't what you give folks to eat so much as 't is makin' 'em feel welcome. Now, there's Mis' Timms; when we was to Longport she was dreadful methodical. She wouldn't let Cap'n Timms fetch nobody home to dinner without lettin' of her know, same's other cap'ns' wives had to submit to. I was thinkin', when she was so cordial over to Danby, how she'd softened with time. Years do learn folks somethin'! She did seem very pleasant an' desirous. There, I am so glad we got started; if she'd gone an' got up a real good dinner to-day, an' then not had us come till to-morrow, 't would have been real too bad. Where anybody lives alone such a thing is very tryin'."

"Oh, so 't is!" said Miss Pickett. "There, I'd like to tell you what I went through with year before last. They come an' asked me one Saturday night to entertain the minister, that time we was having candidates"—

"I guess we'd better step along faster," said Mrs. Flagg suddenly. "Why, Miss Pickett, there's the stage comin' now! It's dreadful prompt, seems to me. Quick! there's folks awaitin', an' I sha'n't get to Baxter in no state to visit Mis' Cap'n Timms if I have to ride all the way there backward!"

III

The stage was not full inside. The group before the store proved to be made up of spectators, except one man, who climbed at once to a vacant seat by the driver. Inside there was only one person, after two passengers got out, and she preferred to sit with her back to the horses, so that Mrs. Flagg and Miss Pickett settled themselves comfortably in the coveted corners of the back seat. At first they took no notice of their companion, and spoke to each other in low tones, but presently something attracted the attention of all three and engaged them in conversation.

"I never was over this road before," said the stranger. "I s'pose you ladies are well acquainted all along."

"We have often traveled it in past years. We was over this part of it last week goin' and comin' from the county conference," said Mrs. Flagg in a dignified manner.

"What persuasion?" inquired the fellow-traveler, with interest.

"Orthodox," said Miss Pickett quickly, before Mrs. Flagg could speak. "It was a very interestin' occasion; this other lady an' me stayed through all the meetin's."

"I ain't Orthodox," announced the stranger, waiving any interest in personalities. "I was brought up amongst the Freewill Baptists."

"We're well acquainted with several of that denomination in our place," said Mrs. Flagg, not without an air of patronage.

"They've never built 'em no church; there ain't but a scattered few."

"They prevail where I come from," said the traveler. "I'm goin' now to visit with a Freewill lady. We was to a conference together once, same's you an' your friend, but 't was a state conference. She asked me to come some time an' make her a good visit, and I'm on my way now. I didn't seem to have nothin' to keep me to home."

"We're all goin' visitin' to-day, ain't we?" said Mrs. Flagg sociably; but no one carried on the conversation.

The day was growing very warm; there was dust in the sandy road, but the fields of grass and young growing crops looked fresh and fair. There was a light haze over the hills, and birds were thick in the air. When the stage-horses stopped to walk, you could hear the crows caw, and the bobolinks singing, in the meadows. All the farmers were busy in their fields.

"It don't seem but little ways to Baxter, does it?" said Miss Pickett, after a while. "I felt we should pass a good deal o' time on the road, but we must be pretty near half-way there a'ready."

"Why, more'n half!" exclaimed Mrs. Flagg. "Yes; there's Beckett's Corner right ahead, an the old Beckett house. I haven't been on this part of the road for so long that I feel kind of strange. I used to visit over here when I was a girl. There's a nephew's widow owns the place now. Old Miss Susan Beckett willed it to him, an' he died; but she resides there an' carries on the farm, an unusual smart woman, everybody says. Ain't it pleasant here, right out among the farms!"

"Mis' Beckett's place, did you observe?" said the stranger, leaning forward to listen to what her companions said. "I expect that's where I'm goin' Mis' Ezra Beckett's?"

"That's the one," said Miss Pickett and Mrs. Flagg together, and they both looked out eagerly as the coach drew up to the front door of a large old yellow house that stood close upon the green turf of the roadside.

The passenger looked pleased and eager, and made haste to leave the stage with her many bundles and bags. While she stood impatiently tapping at the brass knocker, the stage-driver landed a large trunk, and dragged it toward the door across the grass. Just then a busy-looking middle-aged woman made her appearance, with floury hands and a look as if she were prepared to be somewhat on the defensive.

"Why, how do you do, Mis' Beckett?" exclaimed the guest. "Well, here I be at last. I didn't know's you thought I was ever comin'. Why, I do declare, I believe you don't recognize me, Mis' Beckett."

"I believe I don't," said the self-possessed hostess. "Ain't you made some mistake, ma'am?"

"Why, don't you recollect we was together that time to the state conference, an' you said you should be pleased to have me come an' make you a visit some time, an' I said I would certain. There, I expect I look more natural to you now."

Mrs. Beckett appeared to be making the best possible effort, and gave a bewildered glance, first at her unexpected visitor, and then at the trunk. The stage-driver, who watched this encounter with evident delight, turned away with reluctance. "I can't wait all day to see how they settle it," he said, and mounted briskly to the box, and the stage rolled on.

"He might have waited just a minute to see," said Miss Pickett indignantly, but Mrs. Flagg's head and shoulders were already far out of the stage window—the house was on her side. "She ain't got in yet," she told Miss Pickett triumphantly. "I could see 'em quite a spell. With that trunk, too! I do declare, how inconsiderate some folks is!"

"'T was pushin' an acquaintance most too far, wa'n't it?" agreed Miss Pickett. "There, 't will be somethin' laughable to tell Mis' Timms. I never see anything more divertin'. I shall kind of pity that woman if we have to stop an' git her as we go back this afternoon."

"Oh, don't let's forget to watch for her," exclaimed Mrs. Flagg, beginning to brush off the dust of travel. "There, I feel an excellent appetite, don't you? And we ain't got more 'n three or four miles to go, if we have that. I wonder what Mis' Timms is likely to give us for dinner; she spoke of makin' a good many chicken-pies, an' I happened to remark how partial I was to 'em. She felt above most of the things we had provided for us over to the conference. I know she was always counted the best o' cooks when I knew her so well to Longport. Now, don't you forget, if there's a suitable opportunity, to inquire about the drop-cakes;" and Miss Pickett, a little less doubtful than before, renewed her promise.

IV

My gracious, won't Mis' Timms be pleased to see us! It 's just exactly the day to have company. And ain't Baxter a sweet pretty place?" said Mrs. Flagg, as they walked up the main street. "Cynthy Pickett, now ain't you proper glad you come? I felt sort o' calm about it part o' the time yesterday, but I ain't felt so like a girl for a good while. I do believe I'm goin' to have a splendid time."

Miss Pickett glowed with equal pleasure as she paced along. She was less expansive and enthusiastic than her companion, but now that they were fairly in Baxter, she lent herself generously to the occasion. The social distinction of going away to spend a day in company with Mrs. Flagg was by no means small. She arranged the folds of her shawl more carefully over her arm so as to show the pretty palm-leaf border, and then looked up with great approval to the row of great maples that shaded the broad sidewalk. "I wonder if we can't contrive to make time to go an' see old Miss Nancy Fell?" she ventured to ask Mrs. Flagg. "There ain't a great deal o' time before the stage goes at four o'clock; 't will pass quickly, but I should hate to have her feel hurt. If she was one we had visited often at home, I shouldn't care so much, but such folks feel any little slight. She was a member of our church; I think a good deal of that."

"Well, I hardly know what to say," faltered Mrs. Flagg coldly. "We might just look in a minute; I shouldn't want her to feel hurt."

"She was one that always did her part, too," said Miss Pickett, more boldly. "Mr. Cronin used to say that she was more generous with her little than many was with their much. If she hadn't lived in a poor part of the town, and so been occupied with a different kind of people from us, 't would have made a difference. They say she's got a comfortable little home over here, an' keeps house for a nephew. You know she was to our meeting one Sunday last winter, and 'peared dreadful glad to get back; folks seemed glad to see her, too. I don't know as you were out."

"She always wore a friendly look," said Mrs. Flagg indulgently. "There, now, there's Mis' Timms's residence; it's handsome, ain't it, with them big spruce-trees. I expect she may be at the window now, an see us as we come along. Is my bonnet on straight, an' everything? The blinds looks open in the room this way; I guess she's to home fast enough."

The friends quickened their steps, and with shining eyes and beating hearts hastened forward. The slightest mists of uncertainty were now cleared away; they gazed at the house with deepest pleasure; the visit was about to begin.

They opened the front gate and went up the short walk, noticing the pretty herring-bone pattern of the bricks, and as they stood on the high steps Cynthia Pickett wondered whether she ought not to have worn her best dress, even though there was lace at the neck and sleeves, and she usually kept it for the most formal of tea-parties and exceptional parish festivals. In her heart she commended Mrs. Flagg for that familiarity with the ways of a wider social world which had led her to wear the very best among her black cashmeres.

"She's a good while coming to the door," whispered Mrs. Flagg presently. "Either she didn't see us, or else she's slipped upstairs to make some change, an' is just goin' to let us ring again. I've done it myself sometimes. I'm glad we come right over after her urgin' us so; it seems more cordial than to keep her expectin' us. I expect she'll urge us terribly to remain with her over-night."

"Oh, I ain't prepared," began Miss Pickett, but she looked pleased. At that moment there was a slow withdrawal of the bolt inside, and a key was turned, the front door opened, and Mrs. Timms stood before them with a smile. Nobody stopped to think at that moment what kind of smile it was.

"Why, if it ain't Mis' Flagg," she exclaimed politely, "an' Miss Pickett too! I am surprised!"

The front entry behind her looked well furnished, but not exactly hospitable; the stairs with their brass rods looked so clean and bright that it did not seem as if anybody had ever gone up or come down. A cat came purring out, but Mrs. Timms pushed her back with a determined foot, and hastily closed the sitting-room door. Then Miss Pickett let Mrs. Flagg precede her, as was becoming, and they went into a darkened parlor, and found their way to some chairs, and seated themselves solemnly.

"'Tis a beautiful day, ain't it?" said Mrs. Flagg, speaking first. "I don't know's I ever enjoyed the ride more. We've been having a good deal of rain since we saw you at the conference, and the country looks beautiful."

"Did you leave Woodville this morning? I thought I hadn't heard you was in town," replied Mrs. Timms formally. She was seated just a little too far away to make things seem exactly pleasant. The darkness of the best room seemed to retreat somewhat, and Miss Pickett looked over by the door, where there was a pale gleam from the side-lights in the hall, to try to see the pattern of the carpet; but her effort failed.

"Yes, 'm," replied Mrs. Flagg to the question. "We left Woodville about half past eight, but it is quite a ways from where we live to where you take the stage. The stage does come slow, but you don't seem to mind it such a beautiful day."

"Why, you must have come right to see me first!" said Mrs. Timms, warming a little as the visit went on. "I hope you're going to make some stop in town. I'm sure it was very polite of you to come right an' see me; well, it's very pleasant, I declare. I wish you'd been in Baxter last Sabbath; our minister did give us an elegant sermon on faith an' works. He spoke of the conference, and gave his views on some o' the questions that came up, at Friday evenin' meetin'; but I felt tired after getting home, an' so I wasn't out. We feel very much favored to have such a man amon'st us. He's building up the parish very considerable. I understand the pew-rents come to thirty-six dollars more this quarter than they did last."

"We also feel grateful in Woodville for our pastor's efforts," said Miss Pickett; but Mrs. Timms turned her head away sharply, as if the speech had been untimely, and trembling Miss Pickett had interrupted.

"They're thinking here of raisin' Mr. Barlow's salary another year," the hostess added; "a good many of the old parishioners have died off, but every one feels to do what they can. Is there much interest among the young people in Woodville, Mis' Flagg?"

"Considerable at this time, ma'am," answered Mrs. Flagg, without enthusiasm, and she listened with unusual silence to the subsequent fluent remarks of Mrs. Timms.

The parlor seemed to be undergoing the slow processes of a winter dawn. After a while the three women could begin to see one another's faces, which aided them somewhat in carrying on a serious and impersonal conversation. There were a good many subjects to be touched upon, and Mrs. Timms said everything that she should have said, except to invite her visitors to walk upstairs and take off their bonnets. Mrs. Flagg sat her parlor-chair as if it were a throne, and carried her banner of self-possession as high as she knew how, but toward the end of the call even she began to feel hurried.

"Won't you ladies take a glass of wine an' a piece of cake after your ride?" inquired Mrs. Timms, with an air of hospitality that almost concealed the fact that neither cake nor wine was anywhere to be seen; but the ladies bowed and declined with particular elegance. Altogether it was a visit of extreme propriety on both sides, and Mrs. Timms was very pressing in her invitation that her guests should stay longer.

"Thank you, but we ought to be going," answered Mrs. Flagg, with a little show of ostentation, and looking over her shoulder to be sure that Miss Pickett had risen too. "We've got some little ways to go," she added with dignity. "We should be pleased to have you call an' see us in case you have occasion to come to Woodville," and Miss Pickett faintly seconded the invitation. It was in her heart to add, "Come any day next week," but her courage did not rise so high as to make the words audible. She looked as if she were ready to cry; her usual smile had burnt itself out into gray ashes; there was a white, appealing look about her mouth. As they emerged from the dim parlor and stood at the open front door, the bright June day, the golden-green trees, almost blinded their eyes. Mrs. Timms was more smiling and cordial than ever.

"There, I ought to have thought to offer you fans; I am afraid you was warm after walking," she exclaimed, as if to leave no stone of courtesy unturned. "I have so enjoyed meeting you again, I wish it was so you could stop longer. Why, Mis' Flagg, we haven't said one word about old times when we lived to Longport. I've had news from there, too, since I saw you; my brother's daughter-in-law was here to pass the Sabbath after I returned."

Mrs. Flagg did not turn back to ask any questions as she stepped stiffly away down the brick walk. Miss Pickett followed her, raising the fringed parasol; they both made ceremonious little bows as they shut the high white gate behind them. "Good-by," said Mrs. Timms finally, as she stood in the door with her set smile; and as they departed she came out and began to fasten up a rose-bush that climbed a narrow white ladder by the steps.

"Oh, my goodness alive!" exclaimed Mrs. Flagg, after they had gone some distance in aggrieved silence, "if I haven't gone and forgotten my bag! I ain't goin' back, whatever happens. I expect she'll trip over it in that dark room and break her neck!"

"I brought it; I noticed you'd forgotten it," said Miss Pickett timidly, as if she hated to deprive her companion of even that slight consolation.

"There, I'll tell you what we'd better do," said Mrs. Flagg gallantly; "we'll go right over an' see poor old Miss Nancy Fell; 't will please her about to death. We can say we felt like goin' somewhere to-day, an' 't was a good many years since either one of us had seen Baxter, so we come just for the ride, an' to make a few calls. She'll like to hear all about the conference; Miss Fell was always one that took a real interest in religious matters."

Miss Pickett brightened, and they quickened their step. It was nearly twelve o'clock, they had breakfasted early, and now felt as if they had eaten nothing since they were grown up. An awful feeling of tiredness and uncertainty settled down upon their once buoyant spirits.

"I can forgive a person," said Mrs. Flagg, once, as if she were speaking to herself; "I can forgive a person, but when I'm done with 'em, I'm done."

V

"I do declare, 't was like a scene in Scriptur' to see that poor good-hearted Nancy Fell run down her walk to open the gate for us!" said Mrs. Persis Flagg later that afternoon, when she and Miss Pickett were going home in the stage. Miss Pickett nodded her head approvingly.

"I had a good sight better time with her than I should have had at the other place," she said with fearless honesty. "If I'd been Mis' Cap'n Timms, I'd made some apology or just passed us the compliment. If it wa'n't convenient, why couldn't she just tell us so after all her urgin' and say in' how she should expect us?"

"I thought then she'd altered from what she used to be," said Mrs. Flagg. "She seemed real sincere an' open away from home. If she wa'n't prepared to-day, 't was easy enough to say so; we was reasonable folks, an' should have gone away with none but friendly feelin's. We did have a grand good time with Nancy. She was as happy to see us as if we'd been queens."

"'T was a real nice little dinner," said Miss Pickett gratefully. "I thought I was goin' to faint away just before we got to the house, and I didn't know how I should hold out if she undertook to do anything extra, and keep us a-waitin'; but there, she just made us welcome, simple-hearted, to what she had. I never tasted such dandelion greens; an' that nice little piece o' pork and new biscuit, why, they was just splendid. She must have an excellent good cellar, if 't is such a small house. Her potatoes was truly remarkable for this time o' year. I myself don't deem it necessary to cook potatoes when I'm goin' to have dandelion greens. Now, didn't it put you in mind of that verse in the Bible that says, 'Better is a dinner of herbs where love is'? An' how desirous she'd been to see somebody that could tell her some particulars about the conference!"

"She'll enjoy tellin' folks about our comin' over to see her. Yes, I'm glad we went; 't will be of advantage every way, an' our bein' of the same church an' all, to Woodville. If Mis' Timms hears of our bein' there, she'll see we had reason, an' knew of a place to go. Well, I needn't have brought this old bag!"

Miss Pickett gave her companion a quick resentful glance, which was followed by one of triumph directed at the dust that was collecting on the shoulders of the best black cashmere; then she looked at the bag on the front seat, and suddenly felt illuminated with the suspicion that

SARAH ORNE JEWETT

Mrs. Flagg had secretly made preparations to pass the night in Baxter. The bag looked plump, as if it held much more than the pocket-book and the jelly.

Mrs. Flagg looked up with unusual humility. "I did think about that jelly," she said, as if Miss Pickett had openly reproached her. "I was afraid it might look as if I was tryin' to pay Nancy for her kindness."

"Well, I don't know," said Cynthia; "I guess she'd been pleased. She'd thought you just brought her over a little present: but I do' know as 't would been any good to her after all; she'd thought so much of it, comin' from you, that she'd kep' it till 't was all candied." But Mrs. Flagg didn't look exactly pleased by this unexpected compliment, and her fellow-traveler colored with confusion and a sudden feeling that she had shown undue forwardness.

Presently they remembered the Beckett house, to their great relief, and, as they approached, Mrs. Flagg reached over and moved her hand-bag from the front seat to make room for another passenger. But nobody came out to stop the stage, and they saw the unexpected guest sitting by one of the front windows comfortably swaying a palm-leaf fan, and rocking to and fro in calm content. They shrank back into their corners, and tried not to be seen. Mrs. Flagg's face grew very red.

"She got in, didn't she?" said Miss Pickett, snipping her words angrily, as if her lips were scissors. Then she heard a call, and bent forward to see Mrs. Beckett herself appear in the front doorway, very smiling and eager to stop the stage.

The driver was only too ready to stop his horses. "Got a passenger for me to carry back, ain't ye?" said he facetiously. "Them 's the kind I like; carry both ways, make somethin' on a double trip," and he gave Mrs. Flagg and Miss Pickett a friendly wink as he stepped down over the wheel. Then he hurried toward the house, evidently in a hurry to put the baggage on; but the expected passenger still sat rocking and fanning at the window.

"No, sir; I ain't got any passengers," exclaimed Mrs. Beckett, advancing a step or two to meet him, and speaking very loud in her pleasant excitement. "This lady that come this morning wants her large trunk with her summer things that she left to the depot in Woodville. She's very desirous to git into it, so don't you go an' forgit; ain't you got a book or somethin', Mr. Ma'sh? Don't you forgit to make a note of it; here's her check, an' we've kep' the number in case you should mislay it or anything. There's things in the trunk she needs; you know how you overlooked stoppin' to the milliner's for my bunnit last week."

"Other folks disremembers things as well's me," grumbled Mr. Marsh. He turned to give the passengers another wink more familiar than the first, but they wore an offended air, and were looking the other way. The horses had backed a few steps, and the guest at the front window had ceased the steady motion of her fan to make them a handsome bow, and been puzzled at the lofty manner of their acknowledgment.

"Go 'long with your foolish jokes, John Ma'sh!" Mrs. Beckett said cheerfully, as she turned away. She was a comfortable, hearty person, whose appearance adjusted the beauties of hospitality. The driver climbed to his seat, chuckling, and drove away with the dust flying after the wheels.

"Now, she's a friendly sort of a woman, that Mis' Beckett," said Mrs. Flagg unexpectedly, after a few moments of silence, when she and her friend had been unable to look at each other. "I really ought to call over an' see her some o' these days, knowing her husband's folks as well as I used to, an' visitin' of 'em when I was a girl." But Miss Pickett made no answer.

"I expect it was all for the best, that woman's comin'," suggested Mrs. Flagg again hopefully. "She looked like a willing person who would take right hold. I guess Mis' Beckett knows what she's about, and must have had her reasons. Perhaps she thought she'd chance it for a couple o' weeks anyway, after the lady'd come so fur, an' bein' one o' her own denomination. Hayin'-time'll be here before we know it. I think myself, gen'rally speakin', 't is just as well to let anybody know you're comin'."

"Them seemed to be Mis' Cap'n Timms's views," said Miss Pickett in a low tone; but the stage rattled a good deal, and Mrs. Flagg looked up inquiringly, as if she had not heard.

SARAH ORNE JEWETT

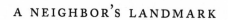

A NEIGHBOR'S LANDMARK

I

The timber-contractor took a long time to fasten his horse to the ring in the corner of the shed; but at last he looked up as if it were a matter of no importance to him that John Packer was coming across the yard. "Good-day," said he; "good-day, John." And John responded by an inexpressive nod.

"I was goin' right by, an' I thought I'd stop an' see if you want to do anything about them old pines o' yourn."

"I don't know's I do, Mr. Ferris," said John stiffly.

"Well, that business is easy finished," said the contractor, with a careless air and a slight look of disappointment. "Just as you say, sir. You was full of it a spell ago, and I kind o' kep' the matter in mind. It ain't no plot o' mine, 'cept to oblige you. I don't want to move my riggin' nowhere for the sake o' two trees—one tree, you might say; there ain't much o' anything but fire-wood in the sprangly one. I shall end up over on the Foss lot next week, an' then I'm goin' right up country quick's I can, before the snow begins to melt."

John Packer's hands were both plunged deep into his side pockets, and the contractor did not fail to see that he was moving his fingers nervously.

"You don't want 'em blowin' down, breakin' all to pieces right on to your grass-land. They'd spile pretty near an acre fallin' in some o' them spring gales. Them old trees is awful brittle. If you're ever calc'latin' to sell 'em, now's your time; the sprangly one's goin' back a'ready. They take the goodness all out o' that part o' your field, anyway," said Ferris, casting a sly glance as he spoke.

"I don't know's I care; I can maintain them two trees," answered Packer, with spirit; but he turned and looked away, not at the contractor.

"Come, I mean business. I'll tell you what I'll do: if you want to trade, I'll give you seventy-five dollars for them two trees, and it's an awful price. Buyin' known trees like them's like tradin' for a tame calf; you'd let your forty-acre piece go without no fuss. Don't mind what folks say. They're yourn, John; or ain't they?"

"I'd just as soon be rid on 'em; they've got to come down some time," said Packer, stung by this bold taunt. "I ain't goin' to give you a present o' half their value, for all o' that."

"You can't handle 'em yourself, nor nobody else about here; there ain't nobody got proper riggin' to handle them butts but me. I've got to take 'em down for ye fur's I can see," said Ferris, looking sly, and proceeding swiftly from persuasion to final arrangements. "It's some like gittin' a tooth hauled; you kind o' dread it, but when 't is done you feel like a man. I ain't said nothin' to nobody, but I hoped you'd do what you was a-mind to with your own property. You can't afford to let all that money rot away; folks won't thank ye."

"What you goin' to give for 'em?" asked John Packer impatiently. "Come, I can't talk all day."

"I'm a-goin' to give you seventy-five dollars in bank-bills," said the other man, with an air of great spirit.

"I ain't a-goin' to take it, if you be," said John, turning round, and taking a hasty step or two toward the house. As he turned he saw the anxious faces of two women at one of the kitchen windows, and the blood flew to his pinched face.

"Here, come back here and talk man-fashion!" shouted the timber-dealer. "You couldn't make no more fuss if I come to seize your farm. I'll make it eighty, an' I'll tell you jest one thing more: if you're holdin' out, thinkin' I'll give you more, you can hold out till doomsday."

"When'll you be over?" said the farmer abruptly; his hands were clenched now in his pockets. The two men stood a little way apart, facing eastward, and away from the house. The long, wintry fields before them sloped down to a wide stretch of marshes covered with ice, and dotted here and there with an abandoned haycock. Beyond was the gray sea less than a mile away; the far horizon was like an edge of steel. There was a small fishing-boat standing in toward the shore, and far off were two or three coasters.

"Looks cold, don't it?" said the contractor. "I'll be over middle o' the week some time, Mr. Packer." He unfastened his horse, while John Packer went to the un-sheltered wood-pile and began to chop hard at some sour, heavy-looking pieces of red-oak wood. He stole a look at the window, but the two troubled faces had disappeared.

SARAH ORNE JEWETT

II

L ater that afternoon John Packer came in from the barn; he had lingered out of doors in the cold as long as there was any excuse for so doing, and had fed the cattle early, and cleared up and laid into a neat pile some fencing materials and pieces of old boards that had been lying in the shed in great confusion since before the coming of snow. It was a dusty, splintery heap, half worthless, and he had thrown some of the broken fence-boards out to the wood-pile, and then had stopped to break them up for kindlings and to bring them into the back kitchen of the house, hoping, yet fearing at every turn, to hear the sound of his wife's voice. Sometimes the women had to bring in fire-wood themselves, but to-night he filled the great wood-box just outside the kitchen door, piling it high with green beech and maple, with plenty of dry birch and pine, taking pains to select the best and straightest sticks, even if he burrowed deep into the wood-pile. He brought the bushel basketful of kindlings last, and set it down with a cheerful grunt, having worked himself into good humor again; and as he opened the kitchen door, and went to hang his great blue mittens behind the stove, he wore a self-satisfied and pacificatory smile.

"There, I don't want to hear no more about the wood-box bein' empty. We're goin' to have a cold night; the air's full of snow, but 't won't fall, not till it moderates."

The women glanced at him with a sense of relief. They had looked forward to his entrance in a not unfamiliar mood of surly silence. Every time he had thumped down a great armful of wood, it had startled them afresh, and their timid protest and sense of apprehension had increased until they were pale and miserable; the younger woman had been crying.

"Come, mother, what you goin' to get me for supper?" said the master of the house. "I'm goin' over to the Centre to the selec'men's office to-night. They're goin' to have a hearin' about that new piece o' road over in the Dexter neighborhood."

The mother and daughter looked at each other with relief and shame; perhaps they had mistaken the timber-contractor's errand, after all, though their imagination had followed truthfully every step of a bitter bargain, from the windows.

"Poor father!" said his wife, half unconsciously. "Yes; I'll get you your supper quick 's I can. I forgot about to-night. You'll want somethin' warm before you ride 'way over to the Centre, certain;" and she began to bustle about, and to bring things out of the pantry. She and John Packer had really loved each other when they were young, and although he had done everything he could since then that might have made her forget, she always remembered instead; she was always ready to blame herself, and to find excuse for him. "Do put on your big fur coat, won't you, John?" she begged eagerly.

"I ain't gone yet," said John, looking again at his daughter, who did not look at him. It was not quite dark, and she was bending over her sewing, close to the window. The momentary gleam of hope had faded in her heart; her father was too pleasant: she hated him for the petty deceit.

"What are you about there, Lizzie?" he asked gayly. "Why don't you wait till you have a light? Get one for your mother: she can't see over there by the table."

Lizzie Packer's ready ears caught a provoking tone in her father's voice, but she dropped her sewing, and went to get the hand-lamp from the high mantelpiece. "Have you got a match in your pocket? You know we're all out; I found the last this mornin' in the best room." She stood close beside him while he took a match from his waistcoat pocket and gave it to her.

"I won't have you leavin' matches layin' all about the house," he commanded; "mice'll get at 'em, and set us afire. You can make up some lamplighters out of old letters and things; there's a lot o' stuff that might be used up. Seems to me lamplighters is gone out o' fashion; they come in very handy."

Lizzie did not answer, which was a disappointment.

"Here, you take these I've got in my pocket, and that'll remind me to buy some at the store," he ended. But Lizzie did not come to take them, and when she had waited a moment, and turned up the lamp carefully, she put it on the table by her mother, and went out of the room. The father and mother heard her going upstairs.

"I do hope she won't stay up there in the cold," said Mrs. Packer in an outburst of anxiety.

"What's she sulkin' about now?" demanded the father, tipping his chair down emphatically on all four legs. The timid woman mustered all her bravery.

"Why, when we saw Mr. Ferris out there talkin' with you, we were frightened for fear he was tryin' to persuade you about the big pines.

Poor Lizzie got all worked up; she took on and cried like a baby when we saw him go off chucklin' and you stayed out so long. She can't bear the thought o' touchin' 'em. And then when you come in and spoke about the selec'men, we guessed we was all wrong. Perhaps Lizzie feels bad about that now. I own I had hard feelin's toward you myself, John." She came toward him with her mixing-spoon in her hand; her face was lovely and hopeful. "You see, they've been such landmarks, John," she said, "and our Lizzie's got more feelin' about 'em than anybody. She was always playin' around 'em when she was little; and now there's so much talk about the fishin' folks countin' on 'em to get in by the short channel in bad weather, and she don't want you blamed."

"You'd ought to set her to work, and learnt her head to save her heels," said John Packer, grumbling; and the pale little woman gave a heavy sigh, and went back to her work again. "That's why she ain't no good now—playin' out all the time when other girls was made to work. Broke you all down, savin' her," he ended in an aggrieved tone.

"John, 't ain't true, is it?" She faced him again in a way that made him quail; his wife was never disrespectful, but she sometimes faced every danger to save him from his own foolishness. "Don't you go and do a thing to make everybody hate you. You know what it says in the Bible about movin' a landmark. You'll get your rights; 't is just as much your right to let the trees stand, and please folks."

"Come, come, Mary Hannah!" said John, a little moved in spite of himself. "Don't work yourself up so. I ain't told you I was goin' to cut 'em, have I? But if I ever do, 't is because I've been twitted into it, an' told they were everybody's trees but mine."

He pleased himself at the moment by thinking that he could take back his promise to Ferris, even if it cost five dollars to do it. Why couldn't people leave a man alone? It was the women's faces at the window that had decided his angry mind, but now they thought it all his fault. Ferris would say, "So your women folks persuaded you out of it." It would be no harm to give Ferris a lesson: he had used a man's being excited and worked upon by interfering neighbors to drive a smart bargain. The trees were worth fifty dollars apiece, if they were worth a cent. John Packer transferred his aggrieved thoughts from his family to Ferris himself. Ferris had driven a great many sharp bargains; he had plenty of capital behind him, and had taken advantage of the hard times, and of more than one man's distress, to buy woodland at far less than its value. More than that, he always stripped land to the bare skin; if the very huckleberry bushes and ferns had been worth anything to him, he would have taken those, insisting upon all or nothing, and, regardless of the rights of forestry, he left nothing to grow; no sapling-oak or pine stood where his hand had been. The pieces of young growing woodland that might have made their owners rich at some later day were sacrificed to his greed of gain. You had to give him half your trees to make him give half price for the rest. Some men yielded to him out of ignorance, or avarice for immediate gains, and others out of bitter necessity. Once or twice he had even brought men to their knees and gained his point by involving them in money difficulties, through buying up their mortgages and notes. He could sell all the wood and timber he could buy, and buy so cheap, to larger dealers; and a certain builder having given him an order for some unusually wide and clear pine at a large price, his withering eye had been directed toward the landmark trees on John Packer's farm.

On the road home from the Packer farm that winter afternoon Mr. Ferris's sleigh-bells sounded lonely, and nobody was met or overtaken to whom he could brag of his success. Now and then he looked back with joy to the hill behind the Packer house, where the assailed pine-trees still stood together, superb survivors of an earlier growth. The snow was white about them now, but in summer they stood near the road at the top of a broad field which had been won from wild land by generation after generation of the Packers. Whatever man's hands have handled, and his thoughts have centred in, gives something back to man, and becomes charged with his transferred life, and brought into relationship. The great pines could remember all the Packers, if they could remember anything; they were like some huge archaic creatures whose thoughts were slow and dim. So many anxious eyes had sought these trees from the sea, so many wanderers by land had gladly welcomed the far sight of them in coming back to the old town, it must have been that the great live things felt their responsibility as landmarks and sentinels. How could any fisherman find the deep-sea fishing-grounds for cod and haddock without bringing them into range with a certain blue hill far inland, or with the steeple of the old church on the Wilton road? How could a hurrying boat find the short way into harbor before a gale without sighting the big trees from point to point among the rocky shallows? It was a dangerous bit of coast in every way, and every fisherman and pleasure-boatman knew the pines on Packer's Hill. As for the Packers themselves, the first great adventure for a child was to climb alone to the great pines, and to see an astonishing world from beneath their shadow; and as the men and women of the family grew old, they sometimes made an effort to climb the hill once more in summer weather, to sit in the shelter of the trees, where the breeze was cool, and to think of what had passed, and to touch the rough bark with affectionate hands. The boys went there when they came home from voyages at sea; the girls went there with their lovers. The trees were like friends, and whether you looked seaward, being in an inland country, or whether you looked shoreward, being on the sea, there they stood and grew in their places, while a worldful of people lived and died, and again and again new worldfuls were born and passed away, and still these landmark pines lived their long lives, and were green and vigorous yet.

III

There was a fishing-boat coming into the neighboring cove, as has already been said, while Ferris and John Packer stood together talking in the yard. In this fishing-boat were two other men, younger and lighter-hearted, if it were only for the reason that neither of them had such a store of petty ill deeds and unkindnesses to remember in dark moments. They were in an old dory, and there was much ice clinging to her, inside and out, as if the fishers had been out for many hours. There were only a few cod lying around in the bottom, already stiffened in the icy air. The wind was light, and one of the men was rowing with short, jerky strokes, to help the sail, while the other held the sheet and steered with a spare oar that had lost most of its blade. The wind came in flaws, chilling, and mischievous in its freaks. "I ain't goin' out any more this year," said the younger man, who rowed, giving a great shudder. "I ain't goin' to perish myself for a pinch o' fish like this"—pushing them with his heavy boot. "Generally it's some warmer than we are gittin' it now, 'way into January. I've got a good chance to go into Otis's shoe-shop; Bill Otis was tellin' me he didn't know but he should go out West to see his uncle's folks,—he done well this last season, lobsterin',—an' I can have his bench if I want it. I do' know but I may make up some lobster-pots myself, evenin's an' odd times, and take to lobsterin' another season. I know a few good places that Bill Otis ain't struck; and then the scarcer lobsters git to be, the more you git for 'em, so now a poor ketch's 'most better'n a good one."

"Le' me take the oars," said Joe Banks, without attempting a reply to such deep economical wisdom.

"You hold that sheet light," grumbled the other man, "or these gusts'll have us over. An' don't let that old oar o' yourn range about so. I can't git no hold o' the water." The boat lifted suddenly on a wave and sank again in the trough, the sail flapped, and a great cold splash of salt water came aboard, floating the fish to the stern, against Banks's feet. Chauncey, grumbling heartily, began to bail with a square-built wooden scoop for which he reached far behind him in the bow.

"They say the sea holds its heat longer than the land, but I guess summer's about over out here." He shivered again as he spoke. "Come, le' 's say this is the last trip, Joe."

Joe looked up at the sky, quite unconcerned. "We may have it warmer after we git more snow," he said. "I'd like to keep on myself until after

SARAH ORNE JEWETT

the first o' the year, same's usual. I've got my reasons," he added. "But don't you go out no more, Chauncey."

"What you goin' to do about them trees o' Packer's?" asked Chauncey suddenly, and not without effort. The question had been on his mind all the afternoon. "Old Ferris has laid a bet that he'll git 'em anyway. I signed the paper they've got down to Fox'l Berry's store to the Cove. A number has signed it, but I shouldn't want to be the one to carry it up to Packer. They all want your name, but they've got some feelin' about how you're situated. Some o' the boys made me promise to speak to you, bein' 's we're keepin' together."

"You can tell 'em I'll sign it," said Joe Banks, flushing a warm, bright color under his sea-chilled skin. "I don't know what set him out to be so poor-behaved. He's a quick-tempered man, Packer is, but quick over. I never knew him to keep no such a black temper as this."

"They always say that you can't drive a Packer," said Chauncey, tugging against the uneven waves. "His mother came o' that old fightin' stock up to Bolton; 't was a different streak from his father's folks—they was different-hearted an' all pleasant. Ferris has done the whole mean business. John Packer'd be madder 'n he is now if he knowed how Ferris is makin' a tool of him. He got a little too much aboard long ago's Thanksgivin' Day, and bragged to me an' another fellow when he was balmy how he'd rile up Packer into sellin' them pines, and then he'd double his money on 'em up to Boston; he said there wa'n't no such a timber pine as that big one left in the State that he knows on. Why, 'tis 'most five foot through high's I can reach."

Chauncey stopped rowing a minute, and held the oars with one hand while he looked over his shoulder. "I should miss them old trees," he said; "they always make me think of a married couple. They ain't no common growth, be they, Joe? Everybody knows 'em. I bet you if anything happened to one on 'em t' other would go an' die. They say ellums has mates, an' all them big trees."

Joe Banks had been looking at the pines all the way in; he had steered by them from point to point. Now he saw them just over Fish Rock, where the surf was whitening, and over the group of fish-houses, and began to steer straight inshore. The sea was less rough now, and after getting well into the shelter of the land he drew in his oar. Chauncey could pull the rest of the way without it. A sudden change in the wind filled the three-cornered sail, and they moved faster.

"She'll make it now, herself, if you'll just keep her straight, Chauncey; no, 't wa'n't nothin' but a flaw, was it? Guess I'd better help ye;" and he leaned on the oar once more, and took a steady sight of the familiar harbor marks.

"We're right over one o' my best lobster rocks," said Chauncey, looking warm-blooded and cheerful again. "I'm satisfied not to be no further out; it's beginnin' to snow; see them big flakes a-comin'? I'll tell the boys about your signin' the paper; I do' know's you'd better resk it, either."

"Why not?" said Joe Banks hastily. "I suppose you refer to me an' Lizzie Packer; but she wouldn't think no more o' me for leavin' my name off a proper neighborhood paper, nor her father, neither. You git them two pines let alone, and I'll take care o' Lizzie. I've got all the other boats and men to think of besides me, an' I've got some pride anyway. I ain't goin' to have Bolton folks an' all on 'em down to the Centre twittin' us, nor twittin' Packer; he'll turn sour toward everybody the minute he does it. I know Packer; he's rough and ugly, but he ain't the worst man in town by a good sight. Anybody'd be all worked up to go through so much talk, and I'm kind o' 'fraid this minute his word's passed to Ferris to have them trees down. But you show him the petition; 't will be kind of formal, and if that don't do no good, I do' know what will. There you git the sail in while I hold her stiddy, Chauncey."

IV

After a day or two of snow that turned to rain, and was followed by warmer weather, there came one of the respites which keep up New England hearts in December. The short, dark days seemed shorter and darker than usual that year, but one morning the sky had a look of Indian summer, the wind was in the south, and the cocks and hens of the Packer farm came boldly out into the sunshine, to crow and cackle before the barn. It was Friday morning, and the next day was the day before Christmas.

John Packer was always good-tempered when the wind was in the south. The milder air, which relaxed too much the dispositions of less energetic men, and made them depressed and worthless, only softened and tempered him into reasonableness. As he and his wife and daughter sat at breakfast, after he had returned from feeding the cattle and horses, he wore a pleasant look, and finally leaned back and said the warm weather made him feel boyish, and he believed that he would take the boat and go out fishing.

"I can haul her out and fix her up for winter when I git ashore," he explained. "I've been distressed to think it wa'n't done before. I expect she's got some little ice in her now, there where she lays just under the edge of Joe Banks's fish-house. I spoke to Joe, but he said she'd do till I could git down. No; I'll turn her over, and make her snug for winter, and git a small boat o' Joe. I ain't goin' out a great ways: just so's I can git a cod or two. I always begin to think of a piece o' new fish quick's these mild days come; feels like the Janooary thaw."

"'T would be a good day for you to ride over to Bolton, too," said Mrs. Packer. "But I'd like to go with you when you go there, an' I've got business here to-day. I've put the kettle on some time ago to do a little colorin'. We can go to Bolton some day next week."

"I've got to be here next week," said Packer ostentatiously; but at this moment his heart for the first time completely failed him about the agreement with Ferris. The south wind had blown round the vane of his determination. He forgot his wife and daughter, laid down his knife and fork, and quite unknown to himself began to hang his head. The great trees were not so far from the house that he had not noticed the sound of the southerly breeze in their branches as he came across the yard. He knew it as well as he knew the rote of the beaches and ledges on that stretch of shore. He was meaning, at any rate, to think it over while he was out fishing, where nobody could bother him. He wasn't going to be hindered by a pack of folks from doing what he liked with his own; but neither was old Ferris going to say what he had better do with his own trees.

"You put me up a bite o' somethin' hearty, mother," he made haste to say. "I sha'n't git in till along in the afternoon."

"Ain't you feelin' all right, father?" asked Lizzie, looking at him curiously.

"I be," said John Packer, growing stern again for the moment. "I feel like a day out fishin'. I hope Joe won't git the start o' me. You seen his small boat go out?" He looked up at his daughter, and smiled in a friendly way, and went on with his breakfast. It was evidently one of his pleasant days; he never had made such a frank acknowledgment of the lovers' rights, but he had always liked Joe Banks. Lizzie's cheeks glowed; she gave her mother a happy glance of satisfaction, and looked as bright as a rose. The hard-worked little woman smiled back in sympathy. There was a piece of her best loaf cake in the round wooden luncheon-box that day, and everything else that she thought her man would like and that his box would hold, but it seemed meagre to her generous heart even then. The two women affectionately watched him away down the field-path that led to the cove where the fish-houses were.

All the Wilton farmers near the sea took a turn now and then at fishing. They owned boats together sometimes, but John Packer had always kept a good boat of his own. To-day he had no real desire to find a companion or to call for help to launch his craft, but finding that Joe Banks was busy in his fish-house, he went in to borrow the light dory and a pair of oars. Joe seemed singularly unfriendly in his manner, a little cold and strange, and went on with his work without looking up. Mr. Packer made a great effort to be pleasant; the south wind gave him even a sense of guilt.

"Don't you want to come, Joe?" he said, according to 'longshore etiquette; but Joe shook his head, and showed no interest whatever. It seemed then as if it would be such a good chance to talk over the tree business with Joe, and to make him understand there had been some reason in it; but John Packer could mind his own business as well as any man, and so he picked his way over the slippery stones, pushed off the dory, stepped in, and was presently well outside on his way to Fish Rock. He had forgotten to look for any bait until Joe had pushed a measure

SARAH ORNE JEWETT

of clams along the bench; he remembered it now as he baited his cod-lines, sitting in the swaying and lifting boat, a mile or two out from shore. He had but poor luck; the cold had driven the fish into deeper water, and presently he took the oars to go farther out, and looking at the land for the first time with a consciousness of seeing it, he sighted his range, and turned the boat's head. He was still so near land that beyond the marshes, which looked narrow from the sea, he could see his own farm and his neighbors' farms on the hill that sloped gently down; the northern point of higher land that sheltered the cove and the fish-houses also kept the fury of the sea winds from these farms, which faced the east and south. The main road came along the high ridge at their upper edge, and a lane turned off down to the cove; you could see this road for three or four miles when you were as far out at sea. The whole piece of country most familiar to John Packer lay there spread out before him in the morning sunshine. The house and barn and corn-house looked like children's playthings; he made a vow that he would get out the lumber that winter for a wood-shed; he needed another building, and his wood-pile ought to be under cover. His wife had always begged him to build a shed; it was hard for a woman to manage with wet wood in stormy weather; often he was away, and they never kept a boy or man to help with farm-work except in summer. "Joe Banks was terribly surly about something," said Mr. Packer to himself. But Joe wanted Lizzie. When they were married he meant to put an addition to the farther side of the house, and to give Joe a chance to come right there. Lizzie's mother was liable to be ailing, and needed her at hand. That eighty dollars would come in handy these hard times.

John Packer liked to be cross and autocratic, and to oppose people; but there was hidden somewhere in his heart a warm spot of affectionateness and desire for approval. When he had quarreled for a certain time, he turned square about on this instinct as on a pivot. The self-love that made him wish to rule ended in making him wish to please; he could not very well bear being disliked. The bully is always a coward, but there was a good sound spot of right-mindedness, after all, in John Packer's gnarly disposition.

As the thought of the price of his trees flitted through John Packer's mind, it made him ashamed instead of pleasing him. He rowed harder for some distance, and then stopped to loosen the comforter about his neck. He looked back at the two pines where they stood black and solemn on the distant ridge against the sky. From this point of view they seemed to have taken a step nearer each other, as if each held the other fast with its branches in a desperate alliance. The bare, strong stem of one, the drooping boughs of the other, were indistinguishable, but the trees had a look as if they were in trouble. Something made John Packer feel sick and dizzy, and blurred his eyes so that he could not see them plain; the wind had weakened his eyes, and he rubbed them with his rough sleeve. A horror crept over him before he understood the reason, but in another moment his brain knew what his eyes had read. Along the ridge road came something that trailed long and black like a funeral, and he sprang to his feet in the dory, and lost his footing, then caught at the gunwale, and sat down again in despair. It was like the panic of a madman, and he cursed and swore at old Ferris for his sins, with nothing to hear him but the busy waves that glistened between him and the shore. Ferris had stolen his chance; he was coming along with his rigging as fast as he could, with his quick French wood-choppers, and their sharp saws and stubborn wedges to cant the trunks; already he was not far from the farm. Old Ferris was going to set up his yellow sawdust-mill there—that was the plan; the great trunks were too heavy to handle or haul any distance with any trucks or sleds that were used nowadays. It would be all over before anybody could get ashore to stop them; he would risk old Ferris for that.

Packer began to row with all his might; he had left the sail ashore. The oars grew hot at the wooden thole-pins, and he pulled and pulled. There would be three quarters of a mile to run up-hill to the house, and another bit to the trees themselves, after he got in. By that time the two-man saw, and the wedges, and the Frenchmen's shining axes, might have spoiled the landmark pines.

"Lizzie's there—she'll hold 'em back till I come," he gasped, as he passed Fish Rock. "Oh, Lord! what a fool! I ain't goin' to have them trees murdered;" and he set his teeth hard, and rowed with all his might.

Joe Banks looked out of the little four-paned fish-house window, and saw the dory coming, and hurried to the door. "What's he puttin' in so for?" said he to himself, and looked up the coast to see if anything had happened; the house might be on fire. But all the quiet farms looked untroubled. "He's pullin' at them oars as if the devil was after him," said Joe to himself. "He couldn't ha' heard o' that petition they're gettin' up from none of the fish he's hauled in; 't will 'bout set him crazy, but I was bound I'd sign it with the rest. The old dory's jumpin' right out of water every stroke he pulls."

V

The next night the Packer farmhouse stood in the winter landscape under the full moon, just as it had stood always, with a light in the kitchen window, and a plume of smoke above the great, square chimney. It was about half past seven o'clock. A group of men were lurking at the back of the barn, like robbers, and speaking in low tones. Now and then the horse stamped in the barn, or a cow lowed; a dog was barking, away over on the next farm, with an anxious tone, as if something were happening that he could not understand. The sea boomed along the shore beyond the marshes; the men could hear the rote of a piece of pebble beach a mile or two to the southward; now and then there was a faint tinkle of sleigh-bells. The fields looked wide and empty; the unusual warmth of the day before had been followed by clear cold. Suddenly a straggling company of women were seen coming from the next house. The men at the barn flapped their arms, and one of them, the youngest, danced a little to keep himself warm.

"Here they all come," said somebody, and at that instant the sound of many sleigh-bells grew loud and incessant, and far-away shouts and laughter came along the wind, fainter in the hollows and loud on the hills of the uneven road. "Here they come! I guess you'd better go in, Joe; they'll want to have lights ready."

"She'll have a fire all laid for him in the fore room," said the young man; "that's all we want. She'll be expectin' you, Joe; go in now, and they'll think nothin' of it, bein' Saturday night. Just you hurry, so they'll have time to light up." And Joe went.

"Stop and have some talk with father," whispered Lizzie affectionately to her lover, as she came to meet him. "He's all worked up, thinking nobody'll respect him, an' all that. Tell him you're glad he beat." And they opened the kitchen door.

"What's all that noise?" said John Packer, dropping his weekly newspaper, and springing out of his chair. He looked paler and thinner than he had looked the day before. "What's all that noise, Joe?"

There was a loud sound of bells now, and of people cheering. Joe's throat had a lump in it; he knew well enough what it was, and could not find his voice to tell. Everybody in the neighborhood was coming, and they were all cheering as they passed the landmark pines.

"I guess the neighbors mean to give you a little party to-night, sir," said Joe. "I see six or eight sleighs comin' along the road. They've all heard about it; some o' the boys that was here with the riggin' went down to the store last night, and they was all tellin' how you stood right up to Ferris like a king, an' drove him. You see, they're all gratified on account of having you put a stop to Ferris's tricks about them pines," he repeated. Joe did not dare to look at Lizzie or her mother, and in two minutes more the room began to fill with people, and John Packer, who usually hated company, was shaking hands hospitably with everybody that came.

Half an hour afterward, Mr. Packer and Joe Banks and Joe's friend Chauncey were down cellar together, filling some pitchers from the best barrel of cider. The guests were tramping to and fro overhead in the best room; there was a great noise of buzzing talk and laughter.

"Come, sir, give us a taste before we go up; it's master hot up there," said Chauncey, who was nothing if not convivial; and the three men drank solemnly in turn from the smallest of the four pitchers; then Mr. Packer stooped again to replenish it.

"Whatever become o' that petition?" whispered Chauncey; but Joe Banks gave him a warning push with his elbow. "Wish ye merry Christmas!" said Chauncey unexpectedly to some one who called him from the stairhead.

"Hold that light nearer," said Mr. Packer. "Come, Joe, I ain't goin' to hear no more o' that nonsense about me beatin' off old Ferris." He had been king of his Christmas company upstairs, but down here he was a little ashamed.

"Land! there's the fiddle," said Chauncey. "Le' 's hurry up;" and the three cup-bearers hastened back up the cellar-stairs to the scene of festivity.

The two Christmas trees, the landmark pines, stood tall and strong on the hill looking down at the shining windows of the house. There was a sound like a summer wind in their tops; the bright moon and the stars were lighting them, and all the land and sea, that Christmas night.

SARAH ORNE JEWETT

ALL MY SAD CAPTAINS

I

Mrs. Peter Lunn was a plump little woman who bobbed her head like a pigeon when she walked. Her best dress was a handsome, if not new, black silk which Captain Lunn, her lamented husband, had bought many years before in the port of Bristol. The decline of shipping interests had cost this worthy shipmaster not only the better part of his small fortune, but also his health and spirits; and he had died a poor man at last, after a long and trying illness. Such a lingering disorder, with its hopes and despairs, rarely affords the same poor compensations to a man that it does to a woman; the claims upon public interest and consideration, the dignity of being assailed by any ailment out of the common course—all these things are to a man but the details of his general ignominy and impatience.

Captain Peter Lunn may have indulged in no sense of his own consequence and uniqueness as an invalid; but his wife bore herself as a woman should who was the heroine in so sad a drama, and she went and came across the provincial stage, knowing that her audience was made up of nearly the whole population of that little seaside town. When the curtain had fallen at last, and the old friends—seafaring men and others and their wives—had come home from Captain Lunn's funeral, and had spoken their friendly thoughts, and reviewed his symptoms for what seemed to them to be the last time, everybody was conscious of a real anxiety. The future of the captain's widow was sadly uncertain, for every one was aware that Mrs. Lunn could now depend upon only a scant provision. She was much younger than her husband, having been a second wife, and she was thrifty and ingenious; but her outlook was acknowledged to be anything but cheerful. In truth, the honest grief that she displayed in the early days of her loss was sure to be better understood with the ancient proverb in mind, that a lean sorrow is hardest to bear.

To everybody's surprise, however, this able woman succeeded in keeping the old Lunn house painted to the proper perfection of whiteness; there never were any loose bricks to be seen on the tops of her chimneys. The relics of the days of her prosperity kept an air of comfortable continuance in the days of her adversity. The best black silk held its own nobly, and the shining roundness of its handsome folds aided her in looking prosperous and fit for all social occasions. She lived alone, and was a busy and unprocrastinating housekeeper. She may have made less raspberry jam than in her earlier days, but it was always pound for pound; while her sponge-cake was never degraded in its ingredients from the royal standard of twelve eggs. The honest English and French stuffs that had been used in the furnishing of the captain's house so many years before faded a little as the years passed by, but they never wore out. Yet one cannot keep the same money in one's purse, if one is never so thrifty, and so Mrs. Lunn came at last to feel heavy at heart and deeply troubled. To use the common phrase of her neighbors, it was high time for her to make a change. She had now been living alone for four years, and it must be confessed that all those friends who had admired her self-respect and self-dependence began to take a keener interest than ever in her plans and behavior.

The first indication of Mrs. Lunn's new purpose in life was her mournful allusion to those responsibilities which so severely tax the incompetence of a lone woman. She felt obliged to ask advice of a friend; in fact, she asked the advice of three friends, and each responded with a cordiality delightful to describe. It happened that there were no less than three retired shipmasters in the old seaport town of Longport who felt the justice of our heroine's claims upon society. She was not only an extremely pleasing person, but she had the wisdom to conceal from Captain Asa Shaw that she had taken any one for an intimate counselor but himself; and the same secrecy was observed out of deference to the feelings and pride of Captain Crowe and Captain Witherspoon. The deplored necessity of re-shingling her roof was the great case in which she threw herself upon their advice and assistance.

Now, if it had been the new planking of a deck, or the selection and stepping of a mast, the counsel of two of these captains would have been more likely to avail a helpless lady. They were elderly men, and had spent so much of their lives at sea that they were not very well informed about shingling their own houses, having left this to their wives, or agents, or some other land-fast persons. They recognized the truth that it would not do to let the project be publicly known, for fear of undue advantage being taken over an unprotected woman; but each found his opportunity to acquire information, and to impart it in secret to Mrs. Lunn. It sometimes occurred to the good woman that she had been unwise in setting all her captains upon the same course, especially as she really thought that the old cedar shingles might last, with judicious patching, for two or three years more.

But, in spite of this weakness of tactics, she was equal to her small campaign.

It now becomes necessary that the reader should have some closer acquaintance with the captains themselves; and to that end confession must be made of the author's belief in a theory of psychological misfits, or the occasional occupation of large-sized material bodies by small-sized spiritual tenants, and the opposite of this, by which small shapes of clay are sometimes animated in the noblest way by lofty souls. This was the case with Captain Witherspoon, who, not being much above five feet in height, bore himself like a giant, and carried a cane that was far too tall for him. Not so Captain Crowe, who, being considerably over six feet, was small-voiced and easily embarrassed, besides being so unconscious of the strength and size of his great body that he usually bore the mark of a blow on his forehead, to show that he had lately attempted to go through a door that was too low. He accounted for himself only as far as his eyes, and in groping between decks, or under garret or storehouse eaves, the poor man was constantly exposing the superfluous portion of his frame to severe usage. His hats were always more or less damaged. He was altogether unaware of the natural dignity of his appearance, and bore himself with great honesty and simplicity, as became a small and timid person. But little Captain Witherspoon had a heart of fire. He spoke in a loud and hearty voice. He was called "The Captain" by his townsfolk, while other shipmasters, active or retired, were given their full and distinctive names of Captain Crowe, Captain Eli Proudfit, or Captain Asa Shaw, as the case might be.

Captain Asa Shaw was another aspirant for the hand of Mrs. Maria Lunn. He had a great deal more money than his rivals, and was the owner of a tugboat, which brought a good addition to his income, since Longport was at the mouth of a river on which there was still considerable traffic. He lacked the dignity and elegance of leisure which belonged to Captains Crowe and Witherspoon, but the fact was patent that he was a younger man than they by half a dozen years. He was not a member of one of the old Longport families, and belonged to a less eminent social level. His straight-forwardness of behavior and excellent business position were his chief claims, besides the fact that he was not only rich, but growing richer every day. His drawbacks were the carping relatives of his late wife, and his four unruly children. Captain Crowe felt himself assured of success in his suit, because he was by no means a poor man, and because he owned the best house in town, over which any woman might be proud to reign as mistress; but he had the defect of owing a home to two maiden sisters who were envious and uneasy at the very suggestion of his marrying again. They constantly deplored the loss of their sister-in-law, and paid assiduous and open respect to her memory in every possible way. It seemed certain that as long as they could continue the captain's habit of visiting her grave, in their company, on pleasant Sundays, he was in little danger of providing a successor to reign over them. They had been very critical and hard-hearted to the meek little woman while she was alive, and their later conduct may possibly have been moved by repentance.

As for the third admirer of Mrs. Lunn, Captain Witherspoon, he was an unencumbered bachelor who had always dreamed of marrying, but had never wished to marry any one in particular until Maria Lunn had engaged his late-blossoming affections. He had only a slender estate, but was sure that if they had been able to get along apart, they could get on all the better together. His lonely habitation was with a deaf, widowed cousin; his hopes were great that he was near to having that happy home of his own of which he had dreamed on land and sea ever since he was a boy. He was young at heart, and an ardent lover, this red-faced little old captain, who walked in the Longport streets as if he were another Lord Nelson, afraid of nobody, and equal to his fortunes.

To him, who had long admired her in secret, Maria Lunn's confidence in regard to the renewing of her cedar shingles had been a golden joy. He could hardly help singing as he walked, at this proof of her confidence and esteem, and the mellowing effect of an eleven o'clock glass of refreshment put his willing tongue in daily danger of telling his hopes to a mixed but assuredly interested company. As he walked by the Lunn house, on his way to and from the harbor side, he looked at it with a feeling of relationship and love; he admired the clean white curtains at the windows, he envied the plump tortoise-shell cat on the side doorstep; if he saw the composed and pleasant face of Maria glancing up from her sewing, he swept his hat through the air with as gallant a bow as Longport had ever seen, and blushed with joy and pride. Maria Lunn owned to herself that she liked him best, as far as he himself was concerned; while she invariably settled it with her judicious affections that she must never think of encouraging the captain, who, like herself, was too poor already. Put to the final test, he was found wanting; he was no man of business, and had lost both his own patrimony and early savings in disastrous shipping enterprises, and still liked to throw down his money to any one who was willing to pick it up. But sometimes, when she saw him pass with a little troop of children at his heels, on their happy way to the candy-shop at the corner, she could not forbear a sigh, or to say to herself, with a smile, that the little man was good-hearted, or that there was nobody who made himself better company; perhaps he would stop in for a minute as he came up the street again at noon. Her sewing was not making, but mending, in these days; and the more she had to mend, the more she sat by one of her front windows, where the light was good.

II

One evening toward the end of summer there came a loud rap at the knocker of Mrs. Lunn's front door. It was the summons of Captain Asa Shaw, who sought a quiet haven from the discomforts of the society of his sisters-in-law and his notoriously ill-bred children. Captain Shaw was prosperous, if not happy; he had been figuring up accounts that rainy afternoon, and found himself in good case. He looked burly and commonplace and insistent as he stood on the front doorstep, and thought Mrs. Lunn was long in coming. At the same moment when she had just made her appearance with a set smile, and a little extra color in her cheeks, from having hastily taken off her apron and tossed it into the sitting-room closet, and smoothed her satin-like black hair on the way, there was another loud rap on the smaller side-door knocker.

"There must be somebody wanting to speak with me on an errand," she prettily apologized, as she offered Captain Shaw the best rocking-chair. The side door opened into a tiny entry-way at the other end of the room, and she unfastened the bolt impatiently. "Oh, walk right in, Cap'n Crowe!" she was presently heard to exclaim; but there was a note of embarrassment in her tone, and a look of provocation on her face, as the big shipmaster lumbered after her into the sitting-room. Captain Shaw had taken the large chair, and the newcomer was but poorly accommodated on a smaller one with a cane seat. The walls of the old Lunn house were low, and his head seemed in danger of knocking itself; he was clumsier and bigger than ever in this moment of dismay. His sisters had worn his patience past endurance, and he had it in mind to come to a distinct understanding with Mrs. Lunn that very night.

Captain Shaw was in his every-day clothes, which lost him a point in Mrs. Lunn's observant eyes; but Captain Crowe had paid her the honor of putting on his best coat for this evening visit. She thought at first that he had even changed his shirt, but upon reflection remembered that this could not be taken as a special recognition of her charms, it being Wednesday night. On the wharves, or in a down-town office, the two men were by way of being good friends, but at this moment great Captain Crowe openly despised his social inferior, and after a formal recognition of his unwelcome presence ignored him with unusual bravery, and addressed Mrs. Lunn with grave politeness. He was dimly conscious of the younger and lesser man's being for some unexplainable reason a formidable rival, and tried blunderingly to show the degree of intimacy which existed between himself and the lady.

"I just looked in to report about our little matter of business. I've got the estimates with me, but 't will do just as well another time," said the big mariner in his disapproving, soft voice.

Captain Shaw instinctively scuffed his feet at the sound, and even felt for his account-book in an inside pocket to reassure himself of his financial standing. "I could buy him an' sell him twice over," he muttered angrily, as loud as he dared.

Mrs. Lunn rose to a command of the occasion at once; there was no sense in men of their age behaving like schoolboys. "Oh, my, yes!" she hastened to say, as she rose with a simpering smile. "'T ain't as if 't was any kind o' consequence, you know; not but what I'm just as much obliged."

Captain Crowe scowled now; this was still the affair of the shingles, and it had been of enough consequence two days before to protract a conversation through two long hours. He had wished ever since that he had thought then to tell Mrs. Lunn that if she would just say the word, she never need think of those shingles again, nor of the cost of them. It would have been a pretty way to convey the state of his feelings toward her; but he had lost the opportunity, it might be forever. To use his own expression, he now put about and steered a new course.

"I come by your house just now," he said to Captain Shaw, who still glowered from the rocking-chair. "Your young folks seemed to be havin' a great time. Well, I like to see young folks happy. They generally be," he chuckled maliciously; "'tis we old ones have the worst of it, soon as they begin to want to have everything their way."

"I don't allow no trouble for'ard when I'm on deck," said Shipmaster Shaw more cheerfully; he hardly recognized the covert allusion to his drawbacks as a suitor. "I like to give 'em their liberty. To-night they were bound on some sort of a racket—they got some other young folks in; but gen'ally they do pretty well. I'm goin' to take my oldest boy right into the office, first o' January—put him right to business. I need more help; I've got too much now for me an' Decket to handle, though Decket's a good accountant."

"Well, I'm glad I'm out of it," said Captain Crowe. "I don't want the bother o' business. I don't need to slave."

"No; you shouldn't have too much to carry at your time o' life," rejoined his friend, in a tone that was anything but soothing; and at this moment Maria Lunn returned with her best lamp in full brilliancy. She had listened eagerly to their exchange of compliments, and thought it would be wise to change the subject.

"What's been goin' on down street today?" she asked. "I haven't had occasion to go out, and I don't have anybody to bring me the news, as I used to."

"Here's Cap'n Shaw makin' me out to be old enough to be his grandfather," insisted Captain Crowe, laughing gently, as if he had taken it as a joke. "Now, everybody knows I ain't but five years the oldest. Shaw, you mustn't be settin' up for a young dandy. I've had a good deal more sea service than you. I believe you never went out on a long voyage round the Cape or the like o' that; those long voyages count a man two years to one, if they're hard passages."

"No; I only made some few trips; the rest you might call coastin'," said Captain Shaw handsomely. The two men felt more at ease and reasonable with this familiar subject of experience and discussion. "I come to the conclusion I'd better stop ashore. If I could ever have found me a smart, dependable crew, I might have followed the sea longer than I did."

It was in the big captain's heart to say, "Poor master, poor crew;" but he refrained. It had been well known that in spite of Shaw's ability as a money-maker on shore, he was no seaman, and never had been. Mrs. Lunn was sure to have heard his defects commented on, but she sat by the table, smiling, and gave no sign, though Captain Crowe looked at her eagerly for a glance of understanding and contempt.

There was a moment of silence, and nobody seemed to know what to say next. Mrs. Maria Lunn was not a great talker in company, although so delightful in confidence and consultation. She wished now, from the bottom of her heart, that one of her admirers would go away; but at this instant there was a loud tapping at a back door in the farther end of the house.

"I thought I heard somebody knocking a few minutes ago." Captain Crowe rose like a buoy against the ceiling. "Here, now, I'm goin' to the door for you, Mis' Lunn; there may be a tramp or somethin'."

"Oh, no," said the little woman, anxiously bustling past him, and lifting the hand-lamp as she went. "I guess it's only Dimmett's been sick"—The last words were nearly lost in the distance, and in the draught a door closed after her, and the two captains were left alone. Some minutes went by before they suddenly heard the sound of a familiar voice.

SARAH ORNE JEWETT

"I don't know but what I will, after all, step in an' set down for just a minute," said the hearty voice of little Captain Witherspoon. "I'll just wash my hands here at the sink, if you'll let me, same 's I did the other day. I shouldn't have bothered you so late about a mere fish, but they was such prime mackerel, an' I thought like's not one of 'em would make you a breakfast."

"You're always very considerate," answered Mrs. Lunn, in spite of what she felt to be a real emergency. She was very fond of mackerel, and these were the first of the season. "Walk right in, Cap'n Witherspoon, when you get ready. You'll find some o' your friends. 'Tis 'The Cap'n,' gentlemen," she added, in a pleased tone, as she rejoined her earlier guests.

If Captain Witherspoon had also indulged a hope of finding his love alone, he made no sign; it would be beneath so valiant and gallant a man to show defeat. He shook hands with both his friends as if he had not seen them for a fortnight, and then drew one of the Windsor chairs forward, forcing the two companions into something like a social circle.

"What's the news?" he demanded. "Anything heard from the new minister yet, Crowe? I suppose, though, the ladies are likely to hear of those matters first."

Mrs. Lunn was grateful to this promoter of friendly intercourse. "Yes, sir," she answered quickly; "I was told, just before tea, that he had written to Deacon Torby that he felt moved to accept the call."

Her eyes shone with pleasure at having this piece of news. She had been thinking a great deal about it just before the two captains came in, but their mutual dismay had been such an infliction that for once she had been in danger of forgetting her best resources. Now, with the interest of these parishioners in their new minister, the propriety, not to say the enjoyment, of the rest of the evening was secure. Captain Witherspoon went away earliest, as cheerfully as he had come; and Captain Shaw rose and followed him for the sake of having company along the street. Captain Crowe lingered a few moments, so obtrusively that he seemed to fill the whole sitting-room, while he talked about unimportant matters; and at last Mrs. Lunn knocked a large flat book off the end of the sofa for no other reason than to tell him that it was one of Captain Witherspoon's old log-books which she had taken great pleasure in reading. She did not explain that it was asked for because of other records; her late husband had also been in command—one voyage—of the ship Mary Susan.

Captain Crowe went grumbling away down the street. "I've seen his plaguy logs; and what she can find, I don't see. There ain't nothin' to a page but his figures, and what men were sick, and how the seas run, an' 'So ends the day.'" It was a terrible indication of rivalry that the captain felt at liberty to bring his confounded fish to any door he chose; and his very willingness to depart early and leave the field might prove him to possess a happy certainty, Captain Crowe was so jealous that he almost forgot to play his role of lover.

As for Mrs. Lunn herself, she blew out the best lamp at once, so that it would burn another night, and sat and pondered over her future. "'T was real awkward to have 'em all call together; but I guess I passed it off pretty well," she consoled herself, casting an absent-minded glance at her little blurred mirror with the gilded wheat-sheaf at the top.

"Everybody's after her; I've got to look sharp," said Captain Asa Shaw to himself that night. "I guess I'd better give her to understand what I'm worth."

"Both o' them old sea-dogs is steerin' for the same port as I be. I'll cut 'em out, if only for the name of it—see if I don't!" Captain Crowe muttered, as he smoked his evening pipe, puffing away with a great draught that made the tobacco glow and almost flare.

"I care a world more about poor Maria than anybody else does," said warm-hearted little Captain Witherspoon, making himself as tall as he could as he walked his bedroom deck to and fro.

III

D own behind the old Witherspoon warehouse, built by the captain's father when the shipping interests of Longport were at their height of prosperity, there was a pleasant spot where one might sometimes sit in the cool of the afternoon. There were some decaying sticks of huge oak timber, stout and short, which served well for benches; the gray, rain-gnawed wall of the old warehouse, with its overhanging second story, was at the back; and in front was the wharf, still well graveled except where tenacious, wiry weeds and thin grass had sprouted, and been sunburned into sparse hay. There were some places, alas! where the planking had rotted away, and one could look down through and see the clear, green water underneath, and the black, sea-worn piles with their fringes of barnacles and seaweed. Captain Crowe gave a deep sigh as he sat heavily down on a stick of timber; then he heard a noise above, and looked up, to see at first only the rusty windlass under the high gable, with its end of frayed rope flying loose; then one of the wooden shutters was suddenly flung open, and swung to again, and fastened. Captain Crowe was sure now that he should gain a companion. Captain Witherspoon was in the habit of airing the empty warehouse once a week—Wednesdays, if pleasant; it was nearly all the active business he had left; and this was Thursday, but Wednesday had been rainy.

Presently the Captain appeared at the basement doorway, just behind where his friend was sitting. The door was seldom opened, but the owner of the property professed himself forgetful about letting in as much fresh air there as he did above, and announced that he should leave it open for half an hour. The two men moved a little way along the oak stick to be out of the cool draught which blew from the cellar-like place, empty save for the storage of some old fragments of vessels or warehouse gear. There was a musty odor of the innumerable drops of molasses which must have leaked into the hard earth there for half a century; there was still a fragrance of damp Liverpool salt, a reminder of even the dyestuffs and pepper and rich spices that had been stowed away. The two elderly men were carried back to the past by these familiar, ancient odors; they turned and sniffed once or twice with satisfaction, but neither spoke. Before them the great, empty harbor spread its lovely, shining levels in the low afternoon light. There were a few ephemeral pleasure-boats, but no merchantmen riding at anchor, no lines of masts along the wharves, with great wrappings of furled sails on the yards; there were no sounds of mallets on the ships' sides, or of the voices of men, busy with unlading, or moving the landed cargoes. The old warehouses were all shuttered and padlocked, as far as the two men could see.

"Looks lonesomer than ever, don't it?" said Captain Crowe, pensively. "I vow it's a shame to see such a harbor as this, an' think o' all the back country, an' how things were goin' on here in our young days."

"'Tis sad, sir, sad," growled brave little Captain Witherspoon. "They've taken the wrong course for the country's good—some o' those folks in Washington. When the worst of 'em have stuffed their own pockets as full as they can get, p'r'aps they'll see what else can be done, and all catch hold together and shore up the shipping int'rists. I see every night, when I go after my paper the whole sidewalk full o' louts that ought to be pushed off to sea with a good smart master; they're going to the devil ashore, sir. Every way you can look at it, shippin' 's a loss to us."

At this moment the shrill whistle of a locomotive sounded back of the town, but the captains took no notice of it. Two idle boys suddenly came scrambling up the broken landing-steps from the water, one of them clutching a distressed puppy. Then another, who had stopped to fasten the invisible boat underneath, joined them in haste, and all three fled round the corner. The elderly seamen had watched them severely.

"It used to cost but a ninepence to get a bar'l from Boston by sea," said Captain Crowe, in a melancholy tone; "and now it costs twenty-five cents by the railroad, sir."

In reply Captain Witherspoon shook his head gloomily.

"You an' I never expected to see Longport harbor look like this," resumed Captain Crowe, giving the barren waters a long gaze, and then leaning forward and pushing the pebbles about with his cane. "I don't know's I ever saw things look so poor along these wharves as they do to-day. I've seen six or seven large vessels at a time waitin' out in the stream there until they could get up to the wharves. You could stand ashore an' hear their masters rippin' an' swearin' aboard, an' fur's you could see from here, either way, the masts and riggin' looked like the woods in winter-time. There used to be somethin' doin' in this place when we was young men, Cap'n Witherspoon."

"I feel it as much as anybody," acknowledged the captain. "Looks to me very much as if there was a vessel comin' up, down there over Dimmett's P'int; she may only be runnin' in closer 'n usual on this light sou'easterly breeze; yes, I s'pose that's all. What do you make her out to be, sir?"

The old shipmasters bent their keen, far-sighted gaze seaward for a moment. "She ain't comin' in; she's only one o' them great schooners runnin' west'ard. I'd as soon put to sea under a Monday's clothes-line, for my part," said Captain Crowe.

"Yes; give me a brig, sir, a good able brig," said Witherspoon eagerly. "I don't care if she's a little chunky, neither. I'd make more money out of her than out o' any o' these gre't new-fangled things. I'd as soon try to sail a whole lumber-yard to good advantage. Gi' me an old-fashioned house an' an old-style vessel; there was some plan an' reason to 'em. Now that new house of Asa Shaw's he's put so much money in—looks as if a nor'west wind took an' hove it together. Shaw's just the man to call for one o' them schooners we just spoke of."

The mention of this rival's name caused deep feelings in their manly breasts. The captains felt an instant resentment of Asa Shaw's wealth and pretensions. Neither noticed that the subject was abruptly changed without apparent reason, when Captain Crowe asked if there was any truth in the story that the new minister was going to take board with the Widow Lunn.

"No, sir," exclaimed Captain Witherspoon, growing red in the face, and speaking angrily; "I don't put any confidence in the story at all."

"It might be of mutual advantage," his companion urged a little maliciously. Captain Crowe had fancied that Mrs. Lunn had shown him special favor that afternoon, and ventured to think himself secure.

"The new minister's a dozen years younger than she; must be all o' that," said the Captain, collecting himself. "I called him quite a young-lookin' man when he preached for us as a candidate. Sing'lar he shouldn't be a married man. Generally they be."

"You ain't the right one to make reflections," joked Captain Crowe, mindful that Maria Lunn had gone so far that very day as to compliment him upon owning the handsomest old place in town. "I used to think you was a great beau among the ladies, Witherspoon."

"I never expected to die a single man," said his companion, with dignity.

"You're gettin' along in years," urged Captain Crowe. "You're gettin' to where it's dangerous; a good-hearted elderly man's liable to be snapped up by somebody he don't want. They say an old man ought to be married, but he shouldn't get married. I don't know but it's so."

"I've put away my thoughts o' youth long since," said the little captain nobly. "Though I ain't so old, sir, but what I've got some years before me yet, unless I meet with accident; an' I'm so situated that I never yet had to take anybody that I didn't want. But I do often feel that there's somethin' to be said for the affections, an' I get to feelin' lonesome winter nights, thinkin' that age is before me, an' if I should get hove on to a sick an' dyin' bed"—

The captain's hearty voice failed for once; then the pleasant face and sprightly figure of the lady of his choice seemed to interpose, and to comfort him. "Come, come!" he said, "ain't we gettin' into the doldrums, Crowe? I'll just step in an' close up the warehouse; it must be time to make for supper."

Captain Crowe walked slowly round by the warehouse lane into the street, waiting at the door while his friend went through the old building, carefully putting up the bars and locking the street door upon its emptiness with a ponderous key; then the two captains walked away together, the tall one and the short one, clicking their canes on the flagstones. They turned up Barbadoes Street, where Mrs. Lunn lived, and bowed to her finely as they passed.

O ne Sunday morning in September the second bell was just beginning to toll, and Mrs. Lunn locked her front door, tried the great brass latch, put the heavy key into her best silk dress pocket, and stepped forth discreetly on her way to church. She had been away from Longport for several weeks, having been sent for to companion the last days of a cousin much older than herself; and her reappearance was now greeted with much friendliness. The siege of her heart had necessarily been in abeyance. She walked to her seat in the broad aisle with great dignity. It was a season of considerable interest in Longport, for the new minister had that week been installed, and that day he was to preach his first sermon. All the red East Indian scarfs and best raiment of every sort suitable for early autumn wear had been brought out of the camphor-chests, and there was an air of solemn festival.

Mrs. Lunn's gravity of expression was hardly borne out by her gayety of apparel, yet there was something cheerful about her look, in spite of her recent bereavement. The cousin who had just died had in times past visited Longport, so that Mrs. Lunn's friends were the more ready to express their regret. When one has passed the borders of middle life, such losses are sadly met; they break the long trusted bonds of old association, and remove a part of one's own life and belongings. Old friends grow dearer as they grow fewer; those who remember us as long as we remember ourselves become a part of ourselves at last, and leave us much the poorer when they are taken away. Everybody felt sorry for Mrs. Lunn, especially as it was known that this cousin had always been as generous as her income would allow; but she was chiefly dependent upon an annuity, and was thought to have but little to leave behind her.

Mrs. Lunn had reached home only the evening before, and, the day of her return having been uncertain, she was welcomed by no one, and had slipped in at her own door unnoticed in the dusk. There was a little stir in the congregation as she passed to her pew, but, being in affliction, she took no notice of friendly glances, and responded with great gravity only to her neighbor in the next pew, with whom she usually exchanged confidential whispers as late as the second sentence of the opening prayer.

The new minister was better known to her than to any other member of the parish; for he had been the pastor of the church to which her lately deceased cousin belonged, and Mrs. Lunn had seen him oftener and more intimately than ever in this last sad visit. He was a fine-looking man, no longer young,—in fact, he looked quite as old as our heroine,—and though at first the three captains alone may have regarded him with suspicion, by the time church was over and the Rev. Mr. Farley had passed quickly by some prominent parishioners who stood expectant at the doors of their pews, in order to speak to Mrs. Lunn, and lingered a few moments holding her affectionately by the hand—by this time gossip was fairly kindled. Moreover, the minister had declined Deacon Torby's invitation to dinner, and it was supposed, though wrongly, that he had accepted Mrs. Lunn's, as they walked away together.

Now Mrs. Lunn was a great favorite in the social circles of Longport—none greater; but there were other single ladies in the First Parish, and it was something to be deeply considered whether she had the right, with so little delay, to appropriate the only marriageable minister who had been settled over that church and society during a hundred and eighteen years. There was a loud buzzing of talk that Sunday afternoon. It was impossible to gainsay the fact that if there was a prospective engagement, Mrs. Lunn had shown her usual discretion. The new minister had a proper income, but no house and home; while she had a good house and home, but no income. She was called hard names, which would have deeply wounded her, by many of her intimate friends; but there were others who more generously took her part, though they vigorously stated their belief that a young married pastor with a growing family had his advantages. The worst thing seemed to be that the Rev. Mr. Farley was beginning his pastorate under a cloud.

While all this tempest blew, and all eyes were turned her way, friends and foes alike behaved as if not only themselves but the world were concerned with Mrs. Maria Lunn's behavior, and as if the fate of empires hung upon her choice of a consort. She was maligned by Captain Crowe's two sisters for having extended encouragement to their brother, while the near relatives of Captain Shaw told tales of her open efforts to secure his kind attention; but in spite of all these things, and the antagonism that was in the very air, Mrs. Lunn went serenely on her way. She even, after a few days' seclusion, arrayed herself in her best, and set forth to make some calls with a pleasant, unmindful manner which puzzled her neighbors a good deal. She had, or professed to have, some excuse for visiting each house: of one friend she asked instructions about her duties as newly elected officer of the sewing society, the first meeting of which had been held in her absence; and another neighbor was kindly requested to give the latest news from an invalid son at a distance. Mrs. Lunn did not make such a breach of good manners as to go out making calls with no reason so soon after her cousin's death. She appeared rather in her most friendly and neighborly character; and furthermore gave much interesting information in regard to the new minister, telling many pleasant things about him and his relations to, and degree of success in, his late charge. There may or may not have been air of proprietorship in her manner; she was frank and free of speech, at any rate; and so the flame of interest was fanned ever to a brighter blaze.

The reader can hardly be expected to sympathize with the great excitement in Longport society when it was known that the new minister had engaged board with Mrs. Lunn for an indefinite time. There was something very puzzling in this new development. If there was an understanding between them, then the minister and Mrs. Lunn were certainly somewhat indiscreet. Nobody could discredit the belief that they had a warm interest in each other; yet those persons who felt themselves most nearly concerned in the lady's behavior began to indulge themselves in seeing a ray of hope.

V

Captain Asa Shaw had been absent for some time in New York on business, and Captain Crowe was confined to his handsome house with a lame ankle; but it happened that they both reappeared on the chief business street of Longport the very same day. One might have fancied that each wore an expression of anxiety; the truth was, they had made vows to themselves that another twenty-four hours should not pass over their heads before they made a bold push for the coveted prize. They were more afraid of the minister's rivalry than they knew; but not the least of each other's. There were angry lines down the middle of Captain Asa Shaw's forehead as he assured himself that he would soon put an end to the minister business, and Captain Crowe thumped his cane emphatically as he walked along the street. Captain John Witherspoon looked thin and eager, but a hopeful light shone in his eyes: his choice was not from his judgment, but from his heart.

It was strange that it should be so difficult—nay, impossible—for anybody to find an opportunity to speak with Mrs. Lunn upon this most private and sacred of personal affairs, and that day after day went by while the poor captains fretted and grew more and more impatient. They had it in mind to speak at once when the time came; neither Captain Crowe nor Captain Shaw felt that he could do himself or his feelings any justice in a letter.

On a rainy autumn afternoon, Mrs. Lunn sat down by her front window, and drew her wicker work-basket into her lap from the end of the narrow table before her. She was tired, and glad to rest. She had been busy all the morning, putting in order the rooms that were to be set apart for the minister's sleeping-room and study. Her thoughts were evidently pleasant as she looked out into the street for a few minutes, and then crossed her plump hands over the work-basket. Presently, as a large, familiar green umbrella passed her window, she caught up a bit of sewing, and seemed to be busy with it, as some one opened her front door and came into the little square entry without knocking.

"May I take the liberty? I saw you settin' by the window this wet day," said Captain Shaw.

"Walk right in, sir; do!" Mrs. Lunn fluttered a little on her perch at the sight of him, and then settled herself quietly, as trig and demure as ever.

"I'm glad, ma'am, to find you alone. I have long had it in mind to speak with you on a matter of interest to us both." The captain felt more embarrassed than he had expected, but Mrs. Lunn remained tranquil, and glanced up at him inquiringly.

"It relates to the future," explained Captain Asa Shaw. "I make no doubt you have seen what my feelin's have been this good while. I can offer you a good home, and I shall want you to have your liberty."

"I enjoy a good home and my liberty now," said Mrs. Lunn stiffly, looking straight before her.

"I mean liberty to use my means, and to have plenty to do with, so as to make you feel comfortable," explained the captain, reddening. "Mis' Lunn, I'm a straight-forward business man, and I intend business now. I don't know any of your flowery ways of sayin' things, but there ain't anybody in Longport I'd like better to see at the head of my house. You and I ain't young, but we"—

"Don't say a word, sir," protested Mrs. Lunn. "You can get you just as good housekeepers as I am. I don't feel to change my situation just at present, sir."

"Is that final?" said Captain Shaw, looking crestfallen. "Come now, Maria! I'm a good-hearted man, I'm worth over forty thousand dollars, and I'll make you a good husband, I promise. Here's the minister on your hands, I know. I did feel all ashore when I found you'd promised to take him in. I tried to get a chance to speak with you before you went off, but when I come home from New York 't was the first news I heard. I don't deem it best for you; you can't make nothin' out o' one boarder, anyway. I tried it once myself."

"Excuse me, Mr. Shaw," said Mrs. Lunn coldly; "I know my own business best. You have had my answer, sir." She added in a more amiable tone, "Not but what I feel obliged to you for payin' me the compliment."

There was a sudden loud knocking at the side door, which startled our friends extremely. They looked at each other with apprehension; then Mrs. Lunn slowly rose and answered the summons.

The gentle voice of the giant was heard without. "Oh, Mis' Lunn," said Captain Crowe excitedly, "I saw some elegant mackerel brought ashore, blown up from the south'ard, I expect, though so late in the season; and I recalled that you once found some acceptable. I thought 't would help you out."

"I'm obliged to you, Captain Crowe," said the mistress of the house; "and to think of your bringin' 'em yourself this drenchin' day! I take it very neighborly, sir." Her tone was entirely different from that in which she had conducted so decisive a conversation with the guest in the sitting-room. They heard the front door bang just as Captain Crowe entered with his fish.

"Was that the wind sprung up so quick?" he inquired, alert to any change of weather.

"I expect it was Captain Shaw, just leavin'," said Mrs. Lunn angrily. "He's always full o' business, ain't he? No wonder those children of his are without manners." There was no favor in her tone, and the spirits of Captain Crowe were for once equal to his height.

The daylight was fading fast. The mackerel were deposited in their proper place, and the donor was kindly bidden to come in and sit down. Mrs. Lunn's old-fashioned sitting-room was warm and pleasant, and the big captain felt that his moment had come; the very atmosphere was encouraging. He was sitting in the rocking-chair, and she had taken her place by the window. There was a pause; the captain remembered how he had felt once in the China Seas just before a typhoon struck the ship.

"Maria," he said huskily, his voice sounding as if it came from the next room,—"Maria, I s'pose you know what I'm thinkin' of?"

"I don't," said Mrs. Lunn, with cheerful firmness. "Cap'n Crowe, I know it ain't polite to talk about your goin' when you've just come in; but when you do go, I've got something I want to send over to your sister Eliza."

The captain gasped; there was something in her tone that he could not fathom. He began to speak, but his voice failed him altogether. There she sat, perfectly self-possessed, just as she looked every day.

"What are you payin' now for potatoes, sir?" continued Mrs. Lunn.

"Sixty cents a bushel for the last, ma'am," faltered the captain. "I wish you'd hear to me, Maria," he burst out. "I wish"—

"Now don't, cap'n," urged the pleasant little woman. "I've made other arrangements. At any rate," she added, with her voice growing more business-like than ever,—"at any rate, I deem it best to wait until the late potatoes come into market; they seem to keep better."

The typhoon had gone past, but the captain waited a moment, still apprehensive. Then he took his hat, and slowly and sadly departed without any words of farewell. In spite of his lame foot he walked some distance beyond his own house, in a fit of absent-mindedness that was born of deep regret. It was impossible to help respecting Mrs. Lunn's character and ability more than ever. "Oh! them ministers, them

SARAH ORNE JEWETT

ministers!" he groaned, turning in at his high white gate between the tall posts with their funeral urns.

Mrs. Lunn heard the door close behind Captain Crowe; then she smoothed down her nice white apron abstractedly, and glanced out of the window to see if he were out of sight, but she could not catch a glimpse of the captain's broad, expressive back, to judge his feelings or the manner in which he was taking his rebuff. She felt unexpectedly sorry for him; it was lonely in his handsome, large house, where his two sisters made so poor a home for him and such a good one for themselves.

It was almost dark now, and the shut windows of the room made the afternoon seem more gloomy; the days were fast growing shorter. After her successful conduct of the affair with her two lovers, she felt a little lonely and uncertain. Although she had learned to dislike Captain Shaw, and had dismissed him with no small pleasure, with Captain Crowe it was different; he was a good, kind-hearted man, and she had made a great effort to save his feelings.

Just then her quick ears caught the sound of a footstep in the street. She listened intently for a moment, and then stood close to the window, looking out. The rain was falling steadily; it streaked the square panes in long lines, so that Mrs. Lunn's heart recognized the approach of a friend more easily than her eyes. But the expected umbrella tipped away on the wind as it passed, so that she could see the large ivory handle. She lifted the sash in an instant. "I wish you'd step in just one minute, sir, if it's perfectly convenient," she said appealingly, and then felt herself grow very red in the face as she crossed the room and opened the door.

"I'm 'most too wet to come into a lady's parlor," apologized Captain Witherspoon gallantly. "Command me, Mrs. Lunn, if there's any way I can serve you. I expect to go down street again this evening."

"Do you think you'd better, sir?" gently inquired Mrs. Lunn. There was something beautiful about the captain's rosy cheeks and his curly gray hair. His kind blue eyes beamed at her like a boy's.

"I have had some business fall to me, you see, Cap'n," she continued, blushing still more; "and I feel as if I'd better ask your advice. My late cousin, Mrs. Hicks, has left me all her property. The amount is very unexpected; I never looked for more than a small remembrance. There will have to be steps taken."

"Command me, madam," said the captain again, to whom it never for one moment occurred that Mrs. Lunn was better skilled in business matters than himself. He instantly assumed the place of protector, which she so unaffectedly offered. For a minute he stood like an admiral ready to do the honors of his ship; then he put out his honest hand.

"Maria," he faltered, and the walls about him seemed to flicker and grow unsteady,—"Maria, I dare say it's no time to say the word just now, but if you could feel toward me"?—

He never finished the sentence; he never needed to finish it. Maria Lunn said no word in answer, but they each took a step forward. They may not have been young, but they knew all the better how to value happiness.

About half an hour afterward, the captain appeared again in the dark street, in all the rain, without his umbrella. As he paraded toward his lodgings, he chanced to meet the Reverend Mr. Farley, whom he saluted proudly. He had demurred a little at the minister's making a third in their household; but in the brief, delightful space of their engagement, Mrs. Lunn had laid before him her sensible plans, and persuaded Captain Witherspoon that the minister—dear, good man! was one who always had his head in a book when he was in the house, and would never give a bit of trouble; and that they might as well have the price of his board and the pleasure of his company as anybody.

Mrs. Lunn sat down to her belated and solitary supper, and made an excellent meal. "'T will be pleasant for me to have company again," she murmured. "I think 'tis better for a person." She had a way, as many lonely women have, of talking to herself, just for the sake of hearing the sound of a voice. "I guess Mr. Farley's situation is goin' to please him, too," she added; "I feel as if I'd done it all for the best." Mrs. Lunn rose, and crossed the room with a youthful step, and stood before the little looking-glass, holding her head this way and that, like a girl; then she turned, still blushing a little, and put away the tea-things. "'T is about time now for the Cap'n to go down town after his newspaper," she whispered; and at that moment the Captain opened the door.

One day, the next spring, Captain Crowe, who had always honored the heroine of this tale for saving his self-respect, and allowing him to affirm with solemn asseverations that though she was a prize for any man, he never had really offered himself to Mrs. Lunn—Captain Crowe and Captain Witherspoon were sitting at the head of Long Wharf together in the sunshine.

"I've been a very fortunate man, sir," said the little captain boldly. "My own property has looked up a good deal since I was married, what with that piece of land I sold for the new hotel, and other things that have come to bear—this wharf property, for instance. I shall have to lay out considerable for new plank, but I'm able to do it."

"Yes, sir; things have started up in Longport a good deal this spring; but it never is goin' to be what it was once," answered Captain Crowe, who had grown as much older as his friend had grown younger since the autumn, though he always looked best out of doors. "Don't you think, Captain Witherspoon," he said, changing his tone, "that you ought to consider the matter of re-shinglin' your house? You'll have to engage men now, anyway, to do your plankin'. I know of some extra cedar shingles that were landed yesterday from somewheres up river. Or was Mis' Witherspoon a little over-anxious last season?"

"I think, with proper attention, sir," said the Captain sedately, "that the present shingles may last us a number of years yet."

A WINTER COURTSHIP

The passenger and mail transportation between the towns of North Kilby and Sanscrit Pond was carried on by Mr. Jefferson Briley, whose two-seated covered wagon was usually much too large for the demands of business. Both the Sanscrit Pond and North Kilby people were stayers-at-home, and Mr. Briley often made his seven-mile journey in entire solitude, except for the limp leather mail-bag, which he held firmly to the floor of the carriage with his heavily shod left foot. The mail-bag had almost a personality to him, born of long association. Mr. Briley was a meek and timid-looking body, but he held a warlike soul, and encouraged his fancies by reading awful tales of bloodshed and lawlessness in the far West. Mindful of stage robberies and train thieves, and of express messengers who died at their posts, he was prepared for anything; and although he had trusted to his own strength and bravery these many years, he carried a heavy pistol under his front-seat cushion for better defense. This awful weapon was familiar to all his regular passengers, and was usually shown to strangers by the time two of the seven miles of Mr. Briley's route had been passed. The pistol was not loaded. Nobody (at least not Mr. Briley himself) doubted that the mere sight of such a weapon would turn the boldest adventurer aside.

Protected by such a man and such a piece of armament, one gray Friday morning in the edge of winter, Mrs. Fanny Tobin was traveling from Sanscrit Pond to North Kilby. She was an elderly and feeble-looking woman, but with a shrewd twinkle in her eyes, and she felt very anxious about her numerous pieces of baggage and her own personal safety. She was enveloped in many shawls and smaller wrappings, but they were not securely fastened, and kept getting undone and flying loose, so that the bitter December cold seemed to be picking a lock now and then, and creeping in to steal away the little warmth she had. Mr. Briley was cold, too, and could only cheer himself by remembering the valor of those pony-express drivers of the pre-railroad days, who had to cross the Rocky Mountains on the great California route. He spoke at length of their perils to the suffering passenger, who felt none the warmer, and at last gave a groan of weariness.

"How fur did you say 't was now?"

"I do' know's I said, Mis' Tobin," answered the driver, with a frosty laugh. "You see them big pines, and the side of a barn just this way, with them yellow circus bills? That's my three-mile mark."

"Be we got four more to make? Oh, my laws!" mourned Mrs. Tobin. "Urge the beast, can't ye, Jeff'son? I ain't used to bein' out in such bleak weather. Seems if I couldn't git my breath. I'm all pinched up and wigglin' with shivers now. 'T ain't no use lettin' the hoss go step-a-ty-step, this fashion."

"Landy me!" exclaimed the affronted driver. "I don't see why folks expects me to race with the cars. Everybody that gits in wants me to run the hoss to death on the road. I make a good everage o' time, and that's all I *can* do. Ef you was to go back an' forth every day but Sabbath fur eighteen years, *you'd* want to ease it all you could, and let those thrash the spokes out o' their wheels that wanted to. North Kilby, Mondays, Wednesdays, and Fridays; Sanscrit Pond, Tuesdays, Thu'sdays, an' Saturdays. Me an' the beast's done it eighteen years together, and the creatur' warn't, so to say, young when we begun it, nor I neither. I re'lly didn't know's she'd hold out till this time. There, git up, will ye, old mar'!" as the beast of burden stopped short in the road.

There was a story that Jefferson gave this faithful creature a rest three times a mile, and took four hours for the journey by himself, and longer whenever he had a passenger. But in pleasant weather the road was delightful, and full of people who drove their own conveyances, and liked to stop and talk. There were not many farms, and the third growth of white pines made a pleasant shade, though Jefferson liked to say that when he began to carry the mail his way lay through an open country of stumps and sparse underbrush, where the white pines nowadays completely arched the road.

They had passed the barn with circus posters, and felt colder than ever when they caught sight of the weather-beaten acrobats in their tights.

"My gorry!" exclaimed Widow Tobin, "them pore creatur's looks as cheerless as little birch-trees in snow-time. I hope they dresses 'em warmer this time o' year. Now, there! look at that one jumpin' through the little hoop, will ye?"

"He couldn't git himself through there with two pair o' pants on," answered Mr. Briley. "I expect they must have to keep limber as eels. I used to think, when I was a boy, that 't was the only thing I could ever be reconciled to do for a livin'. I set out to run away an' follow a rovin' showman once, but mother needed me to home. There warn't nobody but me an' the little gals."

"You ain't the only one that's be'n disapp'inted o' their heart's desire," said Mrs. Tobin sadly. "'T warn't so that I could be spared from home to learn the dressmaker's trade."

"'T would a come handy later on, I declare," answered the sympathetic driver, "bein' 's you went an' had such a passel o' gals to clothe an' feed. There, them that's livin' is all well off now, but it must ha' been some inconvenient for ye when they was small."

"Yes, Mr. Briley, but then I've had my mercies, too," said the widow somewhat grudgingly. "I take it master hard now, though, havin' to give up my own home and live round from place to place, if they be my own child'en. There was Ad'line and Susan Ellen fussin' an' bickerin' yesterday about who'd got to have me next; and, Lord be thanked, they both wanted me right off but I hated to hear 'em talkin' of it over. I'd rather live to home, and do for myself."

"I've got consider'ble used to boardin'," said Jefferson, "sence ma'am died, but it made me ache 'long at the fust on 't, I tell ye. Bein' on the road's I be, I couldn't do no ways at keepin' house. I should want to keep right there and see to things."

"Course you would," replied Mrs. Tobin, with a sudden inspiration of opportunity which sent a welcome glow all over her. "Course you would, Jeff'son,"—she leaned toward the front seat; "that is to say, onless you had jest the right one to do it for ye."

And Jefferson felt a strange glow also, and a sense of unexpected interest and enjoyment.

"See here, Sister Tobin," he exclaimed with enthusiasm. "Why can't ye take the trouble to shift seats, and come front here long o' me? We could put one buff''lo top o' the other,—they're both wearin' thin,—and set close, and I do' know but we sh'd be more protected ag'inst the weather."

"Well, I couldn't be no colder if I was froze to death," answered the widow, with an amiable simper. "Don't ye let me delay you, nor put you out, Mr. Briley. I don't know's I'd set forth to-day if I'd known 't was so cold; but I had all my bundles done up, and I ain't one that puts my hand to the plough an' looks back, 'cordin to Scriptur'."

"You wouldn't wanted me to ride all them seven miles alone?" asked the gallant Briley sentimentally, as he lifted her down, and helped her up again to the front seat. She was a few years older than he, but they had been schoolmates, and Mrs. Tobin's youthful freshness was suddenly revived to his mind's eye. She had a little farm; there was nobody left at home now but herself, and so she had broken up housekeeping for the winter. Jefferson himself had savings of no mean amount.

They tucked themselves in, and felt better for the change, but there was a sudden awkwardness between them; they had not had time to prepare for an unexpected crisis.

"They say Elder Bickers, over to East Sanscrit's been and got married again to a gal that's four year younger than his oldest daughter," proclaimed Mrs. Tobin presently. "Seems to me 't was fool's business."

"I view it so," said the stage-driver. "There's goin' to be a mild open winter for that fam'ly."

"What a joker you be for a man that 's had so much responsibility!" smiled Mrs. Tobin, after they had done laughing. "Ain't you never 'fraid, carryin' mail matter and such valuable stuff, that you'll be set on an' robbed, 'specially by night?"

Jefferson braced his feet against the dasher under the worn buffalo skin. "It is kind o' scary, or would be for some folks, but I'd like to see anybody get the better o' me. I go armed, and I don't care who knows it. Some o' them drover men that comes from Canady looks as if they didn't care what they did, but I look 'em right in the eye every time."

"Men folks is brave by natur'," said the widow admiringly. "You know how Tobin would let his fist right out at anybody that ondertook to sass him. Town-meetin' days, if he got disappointed about the way things went, he'd lay 'em out in win'rows; and ef he hadn't been a church-member he'd been a real fightin' character. I was always 'fraid to have him roused, for all he was so willin' and meechin' to home, and set round clever as anybody. My Susan Ellen used to boss him same's the kitten, when she was four year old."

"I've got a kind of a sideways cant to my nose, that Tobin give me when we was to school. I don't know's you ever noticed it," said Mr. Briley. "We was scufflin', as lads will. I never bore him no kind of a grudge. I pitied ye, when he was taken away. I re'lly did, now, Fanny. I liked Tobin first-rate, and I liked you. I used to say you was the han'somest girl to school."

"Lemme see your nose. 'T is all straight, for what I know," said the widow gently, as with a trace of coyness she gave a hasty glance. "I don't know but what 't is warped a little, but nothin' to speak of. You've got real nice features, like your marm's folks."

It was becoming a sentimental occasion, and Jefferson Briley felt that he was in for something more than he had bargained. He hurried the faltering sorrel horse, and began to talk of the weather. It certainly did look like snow, and he was tired of bumping over the frozen road.

"I shouldn't wonder if I hired a hand here another year, and went off out West myself to see the country."

"Why, how you talk!" answered the widow.

"Yes 'm," pursued Jefferson. "'T is tamer here than I like, and I was tellin' 'em yesterday I've got to know this road most too well. I'd like to go out an' ride in the mountains with some o' them great clipper coaches, where the driver don't know one minute but he'll be shot dead the next. They carry an awful sight o' gold down from the mines, I expect."

"I should be scairt to death," said Mrs. Tobin. "What creatur's men folks be to like such things! Well, I do declare."

"Yes," explained the mild little man. "There's sights of desp'radoes makes a han'some livin' out o' followin' them coaches, an' stoppin' an' robbin' 'em clean to the bone. Your money *or* your life!" and he flourished his stub of a whip over the sorrel mare.

"Landy me! you make me run all of a cold creep. Do tell somethin' heartenin', this cold day. I shall dream bad dreams all night."

"They put on black crape over their heads," said the driver mysteriously. "Nobody knows who most on 'em be, and like as not some o' them fellows come o' good families. They've got so they stop the cars, and go right through 'em bold as brass. I could make your hair stand on end, Mis' Tobin,—I could *so!*"

"I hope none on 'em'll git round our way, I'm sure," said Fanny Tobin. "I don't want to see none on 'em in their crape bunnits comin' after me."

"I ain't goin' to let nobody touch a hair o' your head," and Mr. Briley moved a little nearer, and tucked in the buffaloes again.

"I feel considerable warm to what I did," observed the widow by way of reward.

"There, I used to have my fears," Mr. Briley resumed, with an inward feeling that he never would get to North Kilby depot a single man. "But you see I hadn't nobody but myself to think of. I've got cousins, as you know, but nothin' nearer, and what I've laid up would soon be parted out; and—well, I suppose some folks would think o' me if anything was to happen."

Mrs. Tobin was holding her cloud over her face,—the wind was sharp on that bit of open road,—but she gave an encouraging sound, between a groan and a chirp.

"'T wouldn't be like nothin' to me not to see you drivin' by," she said, after a minute. "I shouldn't know the days o' the week. I says to Susan

Ellen last week I was sure 't was Friday, and she said no, 't was Thursday; but next minute you druv by and headin' toward North Kilby, so we found I was right."

"I've got to be a featur' of the landscape," said Mr. Briley plaintively. "This kind o' weather the old mare and me, we wish we was done with it, and could settle down kind o' comfortable. I've been lookin' this good while, as I drove the road, and I've picked me out a piece o' land two or three times. But I can't abide the thought o' buildin',—'t would plague me to death; and both Sister Peak to North Kilby and Mis' Deacon Ash to the Pond, they vie with one another to do well by me, fear I'll like the other stoppin'-place best."

"*I* shouldn't covet livin' long o' neither one o' them women," responded the passenger with some spirit. "I see some o' Mis' Peak's cookin' to a farmers' supper once, when I was visitin' Susan Ellen's folks, an' I says 'Deliver me from sech pale-complected baked beans as them!' and she give a kind of a quack. She was settin' jest at my left hand, and couldn't help hearin' of me. I wouldn't have spoken if I had known, but she needn't have let on they was hers an' make everything unpleasant. 'I guess them beans taste just as well as other folks',' says she, and she wouldn't never speak to me afterward."

"Do' know's I blame her," ventured Mr. Briley. "Women folks is dreadful pudjicky about their cookin'. I've always heard you was one o' the best o' cooks, Mis' Tobin. I know them doughnuts an' things you've give me in times past, when I was drivin' by. Wish I had some on 'em now. I never let on, but Mis' Ash's cookin' 's the best by a long chalk. Mis' Peak's handy about some things, and looks after mendin' of me up."

"It doos seem as if a man o' your years and your quiet make ought to have a home you could call your own," suggested the passenger. "I kind of hate to think o' your bangein' here and boardin' there, and one old woman mendin', and the other settin' ye down to meals that like's not don't agree with ye."

"Lor', now, Mis' Tobin, le's not fuss round no longer," said Mr. Briley impatiently. "You know you covet me same's I do you."

"I don't nuther. Don't you go an' say fo'lish things you can't stand to."

"I've been tryin' to git a chance to put in a word with you ever sence— Well, I expected you'd want to get your feelin's kind o' calloused after losin' Tobin."

"There's nobody can fill his place," said the widow.

"I do' know but I can fight for ye town-meetin' days, on a pinch," urged Jefferson boldly.

"I never see the beat o' you men fur conceit," and Mrs. Tobin laughed. "I ain't goin' to bother with ye, gone half the time as you be, an' carryin' on with your Mis' Peaks and Mis' Ashes. I dare say you've promised yourself to both on 'em twenty times."

"I hope to gracious if I ever breathed a word to none on 'em!" protested the lover. "'T ain't for lack o' opportunities set afore me, nuther;" and then Mr. Briley craftily kept silence, as if he had made a fair proposal, and expected a definite reply.

The lady of his choice was, as she might have expressed it, much beat about. As she soberly thought, she was getting along in years, and must put up with Jefferson all the rest of the time. It was not likely she would ever have the chance of choosing again, though she was one who liked variety. Jefferson wasn't much to look at, but he was pleasant and appeared boyish and young-feeling. "I do' know's I should do better," she said unconsciously and half aloud. "Well, yes, Jefferson, seem' it's you. But we're both on us kind of old to change our situation." Fanny Tobin gave a gentle sigh.

"Hooray!" said Jefferson. "I was scairt you meant to keep me sufferin' here a half an hour. I declare, I'm more pleased than I calc'lated on. An' I expected till lately to die a single man!"

"'T would re'lly have been a shame; 't ain't natur'," said Mrs. Tobin, with confidence. "I don't see how you held out so long with bein' solitary."

"I'll hire a hand to drive for me, and we'll have a good comfortable winter, me an' you an' the old sorrel. I've been promisin' of her a rest this good while."

"Better keep her a steppin'," urged thrifty Mrs. Fanny. "She'll stiffen up master, an' disapp'int ye, come spring."

"You'll have me, now, won't ye, sartin?" pleaded Jefferson, to make sure. "You ain't one o' them that plays with a man's feelin's. Say right out you'll have me."

"I s'pose I shall have to," said Mrs. Tobin somewhat mournfully. "I feel for Mis' Peak an' Mis' Ash, pore creatur's. I expect they'll be hardshipped. They've always been hard-worked, an' may have kind o' looked forward to a little ease. But one on 'em would be left lamentin', anyhow," and she gave a girlish laugh. An air of victory animated the frame of Mrs. Tobin. She felt but twenty-five years of age. In that moment she made plans for cutting her Briley's hair, and making him look smartened-up and ambitious. Then she wished that she knew for certain how much money he had in the bank; not that it would make any difference now. "He needn't bluster none before me," she thought gayly. "He's harmless as a fly."

"Who'd have thought we'd done such a piece of engineering when we started out?" inquired the dear one of Mr. Briley's heart, as he tenderly helped her to alight at Susan Ellen's door.

"Both on us, jest the least grain," answered the lover. "Gimme a good smack, now, you clever creatur';" and so they parted. Mr. Briley had been taken on the road in spite of his pistol.

A note About the Author

Sarah Orne Jewett (1849–1909) was a prolific American author and poet from South Berwick, Maine. First published at the age of nineteen, Jewett started her career early, combining her love of nature with her literary talent. Known for vividly depicting coastal Maine settings, Jewett was a major figure in the American literary regionalism genre. Though she never married, Jewett lived and traveled with fellow writer Annie Adams Fields, who supported her in her literary endeavors.

A Note from the Publisher

Spanning many genres, from non-fiction essays to literature classics to children's books and lyric poetry, Mint Edition books showcase the master works of our time in a modern new package. The text is freshly typeset, is clean and easy to read, and features a new note about the author in each volume. Many books also include exclusive new introductory material. Every book boasts a striking new cover, which makes it as appropriate for collecting as it is for gift giving. Mint Edition books are only printed when a reader orders them, so natural resources are not wasted. We're proud that our books are never manufactured in excess and exist only in the exact quantity they need to be read and enjoyed.

bookfinity™

Discover more of your favorite classics with Bookfinity™.

- Track your reading with custom book lists.
- Get great book recommendations for your personalized Reader Type.
- Add reviews for your favorite books.
- AND MUCH MORE!

Visit **bookfinity.com** and take the fun Reader Type quiz to get started.

Enjoy our classic and modern companion pairings!

Classic & Modern

Printed in the USA
CPSIA information can be obtained
at www.ICGtesting.com
JSHW022336140824
68134JS00019B/1510

9 781513 279862